THE GNOMOBILE

THE GNOMOBILE

*A Gnice Gnew Gnarrative
With Gnonsense, but Gnothing Gnaughty*

by

UPTON SINCLAIR

ILLUSTRATED BY MARCEL TILLARD

THE **BOBBS-MERRILL** COMPANY, INC.
A SUBSIDIARY OF HOWARD W. SAMS & CO., INC.
Publishers • INDIANAPOLIS • NEW YORK

Library of Congress Catalog No.: 62-19325

FOR ALL WHO LOVE
AND PROTECT OUR FORESTS

CONTENTS

THE GNOMOBILE

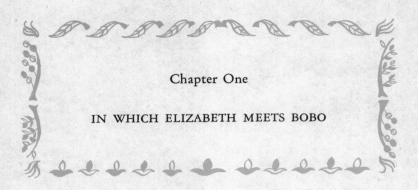

Chapter One

IN WHICH ELIZABETH MEETS BOBO

A little girl was walking in a California forest. It was a forest containing some of the biggest trees in the world, and the little girl had never seen anything like it. She was wandering on, in a sort of daze, hardly able to believe her eyes.

They had been talking in the car about the "big trees," the "giant redwoods." But the words had not meant much to the child. They had been rolling along the highway, twisting and turning on mountain grades, in bright sunlight of a spring day. Suddenly the sunlight was gone, there was twilight and a solemn hush, and a forest made of the largest of living things.

They had stopped and gotten out of the car. Now, by an unusual chance, the little girl was alone with the trees. It would have been no fun with Mama, who would have said: "You will get your shoes dirty," or "There may be rattlesnakes."

By the roadside was a tree with a great hole cut in it. Within was a small restaurant in which you could sit at a table and drink a glass of ginger ale or of soda—"Believe it

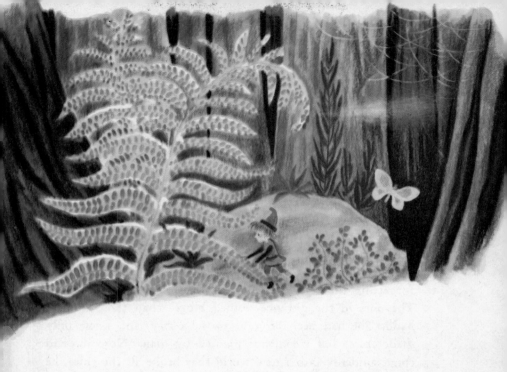

or not," said a sign on the tree. There were picture postcards
of this, and Mama's traveling companion, Miss Jellife, wanted
some to send to friends in the East. Mama was helping her
to choose them; the chauffeur was getting some gas; and so
Elizabeth was left to gaze at the trees and to walk among
them.

Beyond each giant was another, seeming even more marvelous, so that one was drawn on as if by a magic spell. There
were some so big that fifty little girls might have clasped
hands and made rings about their bases. Their bark was gray-
brown and deeply fluted. It looked so soft that you would
think you could squeeze it with your hands, but it was iron-
hard.

13

Under foot was a carpet several feet deep, soft and yielding, made of dust which had dropped from these trees for thousands of years. About the spreading bases of the trees were masses of frail greenery, with faint glimmers of sunlight playing over them—a feeble sunlight, coming from far away, a sun almost played out and dead. Over it all lay a hush as of twilight, of Sunday, the inside of a cathedral—every kind of solemn thing of which you could think.

Beauty and wonder absorbed Elizabeth completely. She went on, softly, reverently, lured by this new sight and that, forgetting the rest of the world. Every tree was different. The ones in the distance seemed bigger than those near at hand. She had been brought up in a city, and knew only shade trees, and woodlands planted by man. Now she had come suddenly into a new world that broke all the rules she had learned.

Thus, she was not really surprised at what happened next. If in this forest there were the biggest of all living things, why should there not also be the smallest? Anything was possible where a hundred million years of history confronted you, and the forces of nature were freed from restraint.

Elizabeth came upon a tree with a great fire-blackened hole straight through it, a hole so big that Mama's limousine could have been driven through without being scratched. She started to peer inside, but it was so dark that it frightened her, and instead she tiptoed around the trunk. On the other side was a rock, over which the tree had grown. On the top of the rock was a fringe of lovely plants—azaleas, and oxalis, and ferns. Peering out over the top of these was a tiny face.

In Which Elizabeth Meets Bobo

It was a face about the size of your fist, unless you have a very big fist. It might have been the face of a squirrel, or of an owl, or of a bear cub. But as it happened, it wasn't any of these—it was a face in all ways human, except that it was so small. It had bright, round, rosy cheeks, tiny blue eyes, hair the color of cornsilk, and above it a tiny little peaked brown cap. It was a startled face, and Elizabeth stopped dead still. The two of them stared at each other.

At last the little man spoke, in a tiny piping voice, "I'm not afraid of you," he said. Elizabeth said quickly, "No, you don't have to be afraid of me."

The little man studied her gravely, and at last remarked, "You look like a very nice person." She answered, "Mama is satisfied most of the time."

The little man studied her some more, and at last inquired, "You do not hurt things?"

"Not if I can help it," said Elizabeth.

"But do you cut down trees?"

"Oh, no! Truly, I have never cut down a tree."

"But you will do it when you grow bigger?"

"No, no, I assure you. Such a thing would not be ladylike."

The little man seemed pleased. "That is a pretty dress you have on," he said next. "Where do you get such things?"

"This came from Marcel's," said Elizabeth. "It is a place on Fifth Avenue." She added, "In New York."

The little man shook his head. "I have lived all my life in this forest. I am very ignorant."

"I am sure," said Elizabeth politely, "you must know lots of things that would be interesting to me."

"I would be glad to tell you," said the little man. He added anxiously, "If I were sure that it is right for me to talk to you."

"Why shouldn't it be right?"

"You are the first big person I have ever spoken to. I have never been allowed to speak to one."

"Who is it that forbids you?"

"Glogo."

"And who is Glogo?"

"He is my grandfather."

"And what is the matter that you cannot speak to big people?"

"He says they are all murderers."

"Oh, surely not!"

"They murder the trees. They destroy the forests, and that is the end of life."

Elizabeth pondered. "I suppose it does seem that way, when you come to think of it," she said. "But please believe me, I have never hurt even the smallest tree. And as for the big ones—how could I, if I wanted to?"

"You will be bigger some day, will you not? You are not a grown-up person. How old are you?"

"I am twelve."

"How strange to think that you should be so big, and yet be only twelve years old!"

"They call me small for my years. How old are you?"

"I just had my hundredth birthday last week."

"And yet you do not look at all old!"

"Glogo is more than a thousand years old."

"Oh, how wonderful! He must be as old as these trees."

"These trees were here before Glogo's grandfather. No one knows how old they are."

Elizabeth looked at the trees again. So they really were as old as they seemed! Her eyes followed the giant columns, which turned red as they ascended—up, up, to the very top of the world. There were spreading branches, and a roof of green, so far away that one could not see what it was made of. There was flickering sunlight, red, green, golden, all magically still, enchanted.

Her eyes came down the trunk again, to the great base—fire-scarred, torn by lightning, patiently repaired by nature with new buttresses, outworks of bark a foot deep. Just beyond was a shattered stump, with new trees growing out of it. Beyond that was a column which had fallen a thousand years ago and lay proof against every form of decay, with only a light crown of ferns along its ridge.

"This is really a most interesting forest," she said, "and I am glad to learn about it. Would you mind telling me what you are?"

"Grandfather says that we are gnomes."

"I have read about gnomes, but I did not know they were real."

"I am quite real," said the gnome.

"I am sure you are very kind and well-bred people. Are there many of you?"

"So far as I know there are only two, Glogo and me."

"Oh, dear me! What has become of the rest?"

"That I do not know. They have disappeared, one and then another. We do not know where they have gone. Glogo says it is because men have cut down the forests."

"That is truly terrible. I never thought about it before."

"Glogo is very sad," continued the gnome. "He is sad about many things and does not tell me the reasons. I have been much worried about him. For a long time I have thought that I should ask some big person for advice. Could you help me?"

"You must understand," explained Elizabeth, "that I am only a child and do not know very much. But I will tell you anything I can."

"Have you ever heard of a person sitting by himself all the time, and looking mournful, and not wanting to eat?"

"Yes, I have," said Elizabeth. "It was that way with my Aunt Genevieve. They had to get all kinds of doctors to advise her. What they call specialists."

"And what did they say?"

"They called it neurasthenia."

"I don't think I could say a word like that," said the gnome.

"It's a way the doctors have," said Elizabeth. "They make up such long words, it frightens you."

"What did they do about your aunt?"

"They did all kinds of things—mud baths, and massage, and baking with electricity, and pills, but it didn't do much good. In the end they told her that she must have a change of scene. Mama said it was because the doctors were tired of her."

"Did the change help her?"

"We don't know. She's in Europe now. She sends us postcards."

"I wonder if it would help Glogo to have a change of scene. We have been in all the forests around here."

18

"I should think that in a thousand years he would have come to know the forests, and everything in them. Maybe he needs a change of diet. What do you eat?"

"We live on fern seed."

"And what do you drink?"

"We drink honeydew from the flowers."

"My, how interesting! It sounds awfully nice. But doesn't it take a lot of time to gather enough fern seed and honeydew?"

"We gnomes have plenty of time."

"Maybe a change of diet would help Glogo. Maybe it would do him good to see the world."

"How could it be done?" asked the gnome anxiously.

The amateur doctor stood in thought. "Let me tell you about my Uncle Rodney," she said. "We are going to visit him and his father—that is, my grandfather—in a big city called Seattle. Maybe you don't know what a city is—it is a place where a great many people live. Rodney is older than I am, but not so very old. He has been to college, and knows a great deal more than I do. Also, he is kind and good. He has never cut down any trees, so perhaps Glogo would not mind meeting him."

"I don't know," said the gnome. "It would be hard to arrange."

"Rodney—I call him that because he says that 'uncle' makes him feel so old—is very good fun. I mean, he says such funny things, he would keep Glogo happy. Another thing, he has some money, and I haven't."

"What is money?"

"Well, it is hard to explain. It is what you get things with—I mean among us people. You would have to have

19

money if you were going to take Glogo to see the world."

The gnome pondered all these ideas. "Would Rodney come to see Glogo?" he inquired.

"I am sure he would. He has probably never met a gnome, and would be much interested."

"I will tell you what I think. It will be better not to say anything to Glogo. He might be very angry; he might go away into the forest, and never be seen again. Let us get Rodney to come and talk it over with me, and we will then find some way for Glogo to meet Rodney by accident."

"Oh, that will be fine!" exclaimed the girl.

"When do you think he will come?"

"We expect to get to the city tomorrow. I will talk to Rodney, and we will come three days from today. If we do not, it will be because he is away, or sick, or something."

"You will surely try to come?"

"Oh, yes, indeed. It is most interesting. It is really educational. Even Mama would admit it—that is, she would if she could believe it. I don't think I shall tell Mama. She says I am imaginative, and would think that I have made you up, and scold me about you."

Elizabeth stopped, as if she thought it was not quite proper for a little girl to know so much about her mother.

At that moment the peace of the forest was broken by the sound of an automobile horn some distance away. "That is the car," said Elizabeth.

"One of those little houses that I see running by so quickly? What is it that makes it go?"

"It is the engine," said Elizabeth. "Rodney will explain it to you better than I can. He has one of his own and will bring me in it. I must go now, or Mama will think that I am lost. She is calling."

Voices were heard in the distance, and Elizabeth put her two hands to her mouth and gave a loud "Yoo-hoo—" a sound which caused the little man to put his fingers in his ears. "My, what a terrifying voice you have!"

"I will use it to call you," replied the girl. "You have not told me what name I shall call."

"My name is Bobo."

"Bobo and Glogo. What pretty names! Mine is Elizabeth."

"That is a long name," said Bobo, and repeated it slowly. "I will learn to say it before you come back. You will surely come?"

"I'll come," called Elizabeth, already running toward the sounds. "Good-by, Bobo!"

The little round face disappeared behind the greenery and Elizabeth hurried as quickly as she could to where the two anxious ladies were waiting. "Oh," cried Mama, "you have ruined your shoes!" And she added, "Don't you know there are rattlesnakes in those woods?" Miss Jellife said, "You might have had a glass of soda inside a tree."

"I am going to learn to drink honeydew inside a flower," replied Elizabeth.

Mama sighed, as they were getting into the car: "The child is so imaginative!"

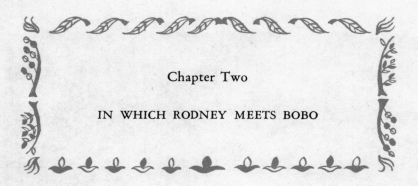

Chapter Two

IN WHICH RODNEY MEETS BOBO

"Old man Sinsabow" was known as one of the lumber kings of the Northwest. He lived in a big palace that he had built out of his own lumber. It was an old-fashioned palace, with bow windows and gables and turrets and towers, showing everything that could be done with lumber. In that palace he had raised a large family and sent it out into the world. Now he was seventy, and his daughters were all married, and two of his sons ran the lumber business, and another ran the family bank, and another the shipping line. They were all worthy of the name of Sinsabow except the youngest, whose name was Rodney.

Rodney did not especially care for lumber or about anything else too much. He made funny remarks about things and about people, including his own family. These remarks somehow made them feel less important—and quite often people do not like that. Old man Sinsabow, who was tougher than the others, would smile grimly now and then. There was nothing about his youngest son that he had any special reason to find fault with—Rodney did not misbehave or get

into the newspapers. He just liked to read books and try to write poetry. The old man thought he could afford to have one son who was different and if Rodney wanted to be a poet, he would buy some newspapers or magazines for him to print his poetry in.

Meanwhile Rodney had an allowance and continued to lounge in his den and read books and make remarks about the lumber business. When he took a friend out driving, he would look at the hills with all the trees cut off, wave his hand and say, "Our northeast turret came from over there." Or he would say, "That is my brother Archie's yacht"—and the visitor might be puzzled by the idea of a yacht on a mountainside. If Rodney saw, in some distant glen, a stand of timber which had not yet been cut, he would say, "That's my next year's allowance."

To this queer uncle came Elizabeth on the evening of her arrival. She tapped on the door and politely asked if she might come in, seated herself in an armchair that was much too big for her, and said: "Rodney, have you ever seen the redwoods? I saw them yesterday for the first time and I didn't see enough of them, because Mama and Miss Jellife were in a hurry. Will you do me a great favor?"

"What?"

"I want to go and see the big trees again. And I'll tell you a secret—at least part of one. I saw something in the forest— I don't want to say what it is, because you couldn't believe me. I just want you to believe that it's something unusual and surprising, and it will make you glad you came."

"In other words," said Rodney, with a smile, "my little niece wants to have a picnic."

"With just you and me, please. Anybody else would spoil it all."

"And when do you want to go?"

"Tomorrow, if you can arrange it. Mama says it's all right, if you won't drive too fast."

So Rodney picked up the telephone, and told the butler that he wanted a thermos bottle full of ice-cold lemonade for Elizabeth and one of hot coffee for himself, and a box of sandwiches and fruit for two, and his car at the door at eight o'clock. Elizabeth was grateful and ever so mysterious.

Next morning they set out on a long drive. But it was not

so long in time, because there were no traffic officers on those hundreds of miles of highway. Rodney had a special kind of car and knew how to drive it specially well. Also he took it for granted that the highways, like everything else, were made for the Sinsabow family.

At noon the next day they came to the place where Mama's car had stopped. They parked and Elizabeth took charge of affairs. She carried the rug to sit on, and Rodney took the basket of lunch, and they went from tree to tree, as Elizabeth remembered her walk of the previous day. They came to the big rock with the fringe of ferns and there they stopped. Elizabeth, with her heart in her mouth, gave a faint little call, "Bobo!" and then a somewhat louder one, "Oh, Bobo!"

Straightway came a shrill little pipe, one syllable at a time, as if the piper were trying to get the name just right, "E-liz-a-beth." Rodney looked startled, and they both peered here and there to see where the sounds came from. The little voice laughed gleefully, thinking it was fun that these big creatures could not see him. In front of them was an old redwood stump, with dozens of little trees starting out from it. Peering between the branches, Elizabeth made out the little round face with the rosy-red cheeks and the little brown peaked cap on top. "Hello, Bobo!" she cried, and then, "This is Rodney. Rodney, let me present my friend Bobo."

"Well, well!" said Rodney, and then again, being at a loss, "Well, well!"

"I didn't tell Rodney about you, Bobo," explained the girl. "I thought he might be afraid of you." And she added: "You see, he is just as nice as I promised."

Bobo pushed out through the fringe of branches, took a seat on the edge of the stump, and surveyed his new visitor. He saw a young man with fair hair and sunburned features, a slightly turned-up nose, and a funny expression which made wrinkles around his eyes.

"Really," said the young man, "this is most interesting. I am ever so glad to make your acquaintance."

"I knew you would be, Rodney. You see, Bobo is a gnome, and has lived in this forest for a hundred years."

"A gnome! Well, I have read about them, of course, but it is the first time I've ever had the pleasure of meeting one. May I ask, Mr. Bobo, is it the custom of your people to shake hands when you are introduced?"

"I have never been introduced before," replied Bobo.

"I do not know how the custom of shaking hands started," said Rodney. "It must have been many thousands of years ago, and I suppose men put out their right hands to each other to show that they had no weapons and did not mean any harm to each other. May I show you how we do it?"

Rodney took the tiny hand very gently in his, and moved it up and down once or twice. Bobo was exactly fourteen and a quarter inches high, and when he was well fed and happy he weighed eleven pounds and fourteen ounces. It was a strange thing to touch his delicate little hand.

"Bobo had never talked with a big person till he met me," explained Elizabeth. "He lives in this forest all alone with his grandfather. They do not know what has become of the rest of their people. They have disappeared, and Glogo— that is his grandfather—thinks it is because the forests have been destroyed."

"Another item to charge against the lumber business," commented Rodney.

"What is the lumber business?" asked Bobo.

"It is the one that cuts down the trees."

"Oh! Then it is a hateful business!"

"Yes, I have long had the same opinion. But my position is an awkward one because it is my family's business. My father is a lumberman and so are some of my brothers."

"How terrible!" The gnome looked as if he wanted to run away.

"Rodney can't help it," pleaded Elizabeth.

"No, Bobo, I assure you. I am the youngest son and a little queer as far as my family is concerned and nothing I do or say counts in the least. My family goes on cutting down trees and if they didn't, other men would, so long as there was a single tree left on the surface of the earth."

A look of horror came upon the gnome's face. "Then Glogo and I are doomed!" he cried.

"No, no," said Rodney hastily. "I said too much. I mean, any trees they can get at. Thank goodness, these redwoods are safe from them. This is a state park and can never be touched. So you and your grandfather will always have a home—and people can come to visit you if you will let them."

"They do not want to be visited, Rodney," explained Elizabeth. "Bobo only spoke to me because he is worried about Glogo."

"What is the matter with Glogo?"

"It seems to be a case of neurasthenia," replied Elizabeth, in her best bedside manner.

"What are the symptoms?"

"Well, he has lost his appetite for fern seed; he sits around and looks sad and does not say much."

"But if he has nobody to talk to but Bobo, I should think he'd have said everything long ago. How old is he?"

"More than a thousand years."

"Mightn't it be just that he is aging, and is tired? Could we have a talk with him?"

"It's not so easy," said Bobo. "He has a dread of the big people and has never let one see him in all his life."

"But can't you explain to him that we are not like most of the others? We love the trees and forests and would not hurt anyone."

"I am afraid he may be angry with me for having disobeyed him. He might disappear into the forest and never let even me see him again."

"My, that *is* a problem!" exclaimed Rodney.

"I have been thinking about it for three days," continued the gnome, "and I have what I think will fix it. I beg you not to be frightened." Then he did a surprising thing. He put his head low down, and drew up his knees, making a sort of ball of himself, and slid off the stump and went rolling. The giant redwoods have a way of spreading out at their bases and the gnome hit one great lump of bark after another and was rolled about on the forest floor. There he lay, while Elizabeth and Rodney gazed in dismay.

"Oh, are you hurt?" cried the girl, running to him.

"A little bit," said Bobo, out of breath. "Quite some, but not too much." Then he sat up and explained. "I would not tell Glogo anything that was not true. But now I can say that I fell out of a tree, and I was hurt, and you picked me up and helped me. So, of course, Glogo cannot blame me and he will have to be polite to you."

"A most ingenious idea!" said Rodney.

"If you will be so good as to carry me now—"

"Oh, let me do it!" exclaimed Elizabeth. Rodney carried

the robe and the lunch basket, while Elizabeth took the little creature into her arms, very carefully, just as if he had been a baby. "How light you are, and how nice to carry, Bobo. You would make a lovely pet!"

"I might bite and scratch if I did not like it," said Bobo. But he seemed to like it and snuggled close and warm, just like a pet.

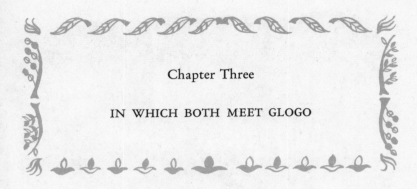

Chapter Three

IN WHICH BOTH MEET GLOGO

Elizabeth, carrying Bobo, and Rodney, carrying the basket, went on deeper into the forest, following Bobo's directions. The ferns grew thicker, and the silence deeper, until at last Bobo said, "Here." Then he whispered, "Don't put me down, because I have been hurt." He raised his shrill little pipe, "Glogo! Glogo!"

There was a long silence. The two big people had no way of knowing that Glogo was anywhere near, but apparently Bobo had some way of knowing, for he began to talk. "Glogo, I fell out of a tree and hurt myself, and these big people have been helping me. They are very good and kind people. They love the trees and help to take care of them, so please forgive me for letting them carry me."

Again a silence and Bobo seemed to find something in it to frighten him, for he went on anxiously, "They are not at all like the other people, Glogo. They have never cut down a tree, and they have been so polite—please forgive them, Glogo."

Again there was a pause, until from somewhere in a big

clump of azaleas came a voice, deeper than Bobo's, and stern, in spite of its lack of volume. "Tell the big people to put you down and go away."

"But, Glogo, that is not polite."

"The big people are never polite. They are murderers."

"No, Glogo, these are very wise people. Rodney is a student and can tell you many things about the world." Again a pause. "Please answer, Glogo."

"I do not want to know anything that the big people have to tell."

"Believe me, Glogo, Rodney knows many useful things. He can tell you about this forest—that it is a state park and will never be destroyed."

"He himself will be destroyed, and his state, and its parks."

Again there was a silence. Bobo began to plead, with fear in his voice—thinking perhaps that these strange big people might take offense and go away. "Believe me, Glogo, these people have ways of learning many things. They have ways of going about—Rodney will take us—to help us to find some other gnomes in some other forest. They really want to help us."

"The gnomes were happy and they did not have the help of the big people. All the big people can do for us is to go away—as far away as possible."

Bobo looked up at Elizabeth and she saw that there were tears in his eyes. Rodney saw it too and took a step forward. "Let me speak," he said. And addressing the clump of azaleas, he began.

"I know that we big people have been very stupid and cruel. There are a few of us trying to change that and having a hard time of it. It may be that we shall fail entirely. I cannot promise. But I have tried in my feeble way. I bought one tract of these redwood forests and gave it to the state to be protected forever. I can take you and show you the place on the highway where my name is written on a bronze plaque. So you ought to be a little grateful to me, Glogo, in spite of my having the misfortune to be born so big."

Said the stern voice out of the azalea clump, "There is nothing I can do for you."

"You are mistaken, Glogo. I am a student and I have been visiting the forests, trying to learn to talk to the trees. You can teach me."

"How do you know I can talk to the trees?"

"I know that no wise person like yourself can live in the forest for a thousand years without learning to talk to all living things. I know that the trees have souls like persons."

35

"They are not at all like persons! Their souls are kind. When did a tree ever make a sharp ax to destroy things? A tree builds. It labors without rest, day and night. It performs mighty labors. It draws the sap up from the ground and builds it into bark and heartwood and branches and leaves."

"Yes, Glogo. And the greatest scientist in the whole world does not know by what means the tree does that. How can a tree know which is the place for bark and which for leaf? By what means does it know that it has been wounded and send the sap to build new bark and new heartwood?"

"A tree knows all the things which a tree needs for its own life and for the life of the future—the billions of precious seeds which it makes."

"How does a tree speak to you, Glogo? Does it use words?"

"A tree has no tongue with which to make words. A tree speaks in actions. If you love it and live with it, its spirit becomes one with yours and you understand it, and hate the madmen who murder it."

"Listen to me, Glogo. You are old and wise, and I am nothing but a child. I have lived only twenty-three years— and what can one learn in that time? I beg you humbly to tell me the secrets of the forest. Perhaps I can go back and teach them to men, and they will be less mad than they have been in the past."

Said the stern voice, after a pause, "You are asking me to break the rule of a million years. It is not only myself, but all the generations of the gnomes who forbid me."

"But, Glogo, if a rule does not work—is not a million years' trial enough? This rule has left only you and Bobo and what is going to become of him when you are gone?"

"Do not say that!" cried the voice from the azalea clump, in what seemed to be anger.

"But it is true, Glogo. What is going to become of the race of gnomes, if you do not find a wife for your grandson?"

There came only a moan out of the bushes.

"You have thought of that, Glogo?"

The answer came, almost in a whisper, "I have thought of nothing else for many years."

"That is why you are so unhappy?"

"I am the most unhappy of living things."

"But Glogo," broke in Bobo, "you don't have to worry about me. I'm not missing a wife."

"Foolish boy," said the voice. "All the future of the gnomes is missing your wife."

A long silence. Said Rodney at last, "I wish I could say that I know where there are other gnomes. But, as you know, they hide themselves from men. All I can say is that I will be your friend if you will let me, and I will do everything in my power to search the forests and find more of your people. I will do that, whether or not you consent to teach me the wisdom of your forest."

For the first time the hidden voice showed signs of weakening. "That is fairly spoken. But do men ever mean what their words say?"

"But," argued the young man, "if we meant harm to you, we already have Bobo in our power. And as for you—when one has lived a thousand years, has he so much to risk?"

"It is true." And suddenly the bushes were parted and there came out a figure of the same size as Bobo, with the same short trousers and little brown peaked cap. But the face of this little creature was longer and had wrinkles in it and a straggly gray beard reaching almost to the waist. "I am here," said Glogo. "I will try to be your friend."

"I thank you, sir," said Rodney, with a grave bow, which the old gnome gravely returned. "My name is Rodney, and this is my little niece, Elizabeth." Again the old gnome bowed.

"And now," continued Rodney, "I think we should make ourselves comfortable so that we may talk." He spread the robe on the floor of the forest, and Elizabeth set Bobo down.

"Are you hurt?" demanded the old one. Bobo answered that he was all right now and proved it by jumping up.

Elizabeth and Rodney seated themselves. Glogo, at their invitation, sat on one corner of the robe—the one nearest to the bushes. From time to time he would glance about him nervously and one could see that he was ready to leap up and dash away at the slightest sign of danger.

"Let me tell you, to begin with," said Rodney, "that I have been a student at what is called a university. May I ask, did you have those among the gnomes?"

"We gnomes did most of our learning day by day, as we lived," said Glogo. "We learned not merely from our elders, but from all things in nature and the spirits of the trees and the plants."

"All trees and plants have spirits, then?"

"All living things have spirits. How else can they act? How can they grow?"

"Are you able to exchange ideas with all these spirits?"

"All living things exchange ideas, even though they may not know it."

"Tell me about the spirit of this fern, for example." Rodney touched one close by his hand.

"The spirit of the fern is like that of a woman," said Glogo. "It is gentle, modest, and humble, but also very strong—nothing discourages it. You have thoughtlessly bent and hurt one. It will suffer in silence but when you are gone it will bravely go on with its task of making beauty. The little girl will understand the spirit of the fern, which hangs curtains all over the forest and cannot rest until it has made the place pretty and homelike."

"That is a very nice way to say it," said Elizabeth. "I think I would understand the spirits of both the ferns and the flowers."

"I suppose," said Rodney, "that one has to be very old indeed in order to know the spirit of one of these redwoods."

"A tree like that speaks of a great victory won. Millions of pounds of matter have been taken out of the earth with careful choice, and dissolved in water, lifted to those tremendous heights, and built into a tower which takes care of itself, and is safe against the blind forces of wind and fire. The spirit which builds that tree is strong and serene—it knows its power. It is in fact a great system in which many spirits work in harmony. It is music which our Mother Nature has played for a hundred million years. And there has come only one voice to disturb it."

"I know what you mean," said Rodney. "There was a wise old man among us who said that God had protected the redwoods against everything but fools."

"I am glad to hear of such a man," replied Glogo. "It makes it easier for me to talk to you."

"Our wise old man added that only the state could protect the trees against the fools. And to some extent, that is being done."

"I fear it is too late for my people," said Glogo, and appeared to sink back into that mournfulness which had caused his case to be diagnosed as neurasthenia.

"We are going to find out about it," said Rodney with the quick cheerfulness that has to be learned by those who attend depressed people. "But first let me explain that it is the hour when we big people are accustomed to have lunch. How is it with you, Glogo?"

"We gnomes do not have regular hours for eating. We take our fern seed when and where we find it."

"I wonder if you would be willing to try some of the kinds of food we have brought with us?"

Elizabeth began to unpack the lunch basket. She spread a paper tablecloth and laid out four folded paper napkins. She took out the box of sandwiches, each wrapped in a piece of wax paper. There were stuffed eggs, and a bottle of olives, and a little box of nuts, some lettuce and tomatoes, several ripe bananas, a bottle of milk, and the two thermos bottles. It was doubtless more food than the two gnomes had even seen piled together in their many years of life. Bobo's quick bright eyes moved from one object to another.

First they must "wet their whistles," said Rodney. A difficulty arose at once, for the cups which they had with them were not of gnome size. "I will fix that," said Bobo, eager to taste all the strange foods of the big people. Forgetting his aches, he ran into the forest and came back with two gleaming tiger lilies. He twisted out the stamens and pistils,

and wiped the cups clean of their golden pollen. Then into each of them Elizabeth poured some lemonade out of the thermos bottle and watched the faces of the two gnomes while they tasted it.

"It is cold as the mountain snows!" exclaimed Bobo.

Not even neurasthenia could hold out against such a surprise. "Is it a spirit?" asked Glogo.

"It might be," answered Rodney. "I have learned from you that there are all sorts of spirits. Here is a different kind," he added, as he poured out the coffee. "Be careful now, for this is a mischievous spirit and he will bite your tongue if he can."

Of course, the butler in the home of a lumber king would see to it that the thermos bottle contained good coffee and the right amount of cream and sugar. Bobo was loud in his cries of delight with the hot beverage, and Rodney explained that it was the spirit of the sun which the big people had learned to pen up in a bottle and take into their stomachs.

He told them how the lemons had come from Southern California, and the sugar from Louisiana, and the coffee from Brazil, and the cream from Wisconsin. All this was not so easy to understand, for the little forest creatures did not know that the earth was so big, and while they had learned that there were oceans, they did not understand how ships could sail upon them. Besides, when you are trying to help an old gnome to be happy, it is a mistake to speak of ships and to have to tell him that many of them are made out of murdered trees.

Elizabeth gave each of them a small piece of sandwich. Rodney had to explain how wheat was grown and ground, and how butter and cheese were made from the milk of cows. Glogo took all this with quiet dignity, but Bobo was full of curiosity and fun, and nibbled his bread and his butter and his cheese, each one separately.

A banana had to be cut into small slices so that he could get comfortable bites out of it. Then Rodney had to tell him about the strange kind of forests in which these plants grew, so differently from the giant redwoods. Yet they were very old plants too. Their ancestors had been on earth for millions of years, and had furnished food for all sorts of people. Some of them were small people, said Rodney, known as pygmies, but they were much bigger than gnomes, and Rodney did not think that Bobo would like to have a pygmy lady for a wife. Besides, she would speak Portuguese, or Indian, or some other language he wouldn't understand.

"By the way," said Rodney to Glogo, "I have been meaning to ask you, how does it happen that your people speak English?"

"English?" said the old gnome. "What is that?"

"That is the name of the language you speak."

"What a strange idea!" commented Glogo. "I had in mind to ask you how you came to speak Gnomic." And so that was that.

Chapter Four

IN WHICH THE GNOMOBILE SETS FORTH

"And now," said Rodney, "the time has come for us to set out on our search."

They talked about gnomes and their habits. There was no use looking in this forest or others close by, because Glogo and Bobo had been all over them. They would go to others of the redwood groves, some distance away. Said Bobo to his grandfather, "Rodney has one of those houses that we see rolling by so quickly. He wants to show us how it goes."

"Is it a spirit that makes it go?" inquired the old gnome.

"I suppose you might call it that," replied Rodney. "It is again the spirit of the sun which we use. Men have learned to imprison the sun and the lightning."

"Nothing should be imprisoned," said Glogo.

"It isn't really imprisoned," said Rodney hastily. "It is allowed to change itself into something else. It is what the trees do—turning one form of life into another."

"What do you call the thing?" asked Glogo.

"We call it an automobile. That means something which

moves itself. When it moves gnomes, I suppose it should
be called a gnomobile."

"Oh, lovely!" cried Elizabeth, clapping her hands. "Such
a lark—to take a trip in a gnomobile."

"But can you be sure it will like us?" asked the cautious
grandfather.

"As soon as it learns that it is a gnomobile," said Rodney,
"it will understand that it is made to carry gnomes." And
he added suddenly: "I think it would be nice to have a
poem about a gnomobile. Wait, please."

In Which the Gnomobile Sets Forth

Elizabeth was familiar with this peculiarity of her uncle's. At the most unexpected moment, he would suggest a poem. Then he liked everybody to be quiet for a minute or two, after which he would recite something. Apparently the gnomes had also had poets among them, for they kept as still as mice. Presently Rodney began,

> I am the gnifty gnomobile,
> Before my gname all gnations gneel;
> I'm gneat and gnice in all my motions,
> But sometimes have agnoying gnotions;
> And when I have a gnut that loosens
> Then I can be a gnawful gnuisance.
> Take gnotice gnot to drive too quick—
> I'll gnock your gnoodle like old Gnick;
> But gnow egnough to gnurse your speed
> And I will gnever fail your gneed.

Elizabeth thought it was a charming poem when she heard it recited. But when she saw it written out, she wondered how could she ever learn to spell all those difficult words.

The next problem was to get to the gnomobile without being seen. Rodney explained that the big people are very excitable and if they saw anything they had never seen before, they would crowd about and stare. Worse yet, the news about the gnomes being found in the forest might get into the papers and after that they would never have any peace. Crowds would rush to the place and Glogo and Bobo would be overwhelmed with what are called "social duties."

"When we take you to the gnomobile," said Rodney, "I

will wrap you in this robe and carry you. I will then put the robe on the seat so that if any big person comes near the gnomobile, you will be able to hide under it."

"We are quite used to hiding," said the old one. "Our lives have depended upon it."

They gathered up the lunch things and put them into the basket, which was now lighter. Rodney made the robe into a sort of sack, in which the two gnomes hid with just their heads sticking out. There was a flap which they could pull over themselves in a hurry. So he carried them to the gnomobile and unlocked it and put them inside on the back seat. There were other cars parked in this place and people walking about, but no one paid any attention to what Rodney was doing.

But a new kind of trouble appeared. Glogo took one look at the inside of the gnomobile and his eye fell upon the trim of the window. Thereupon he sank down on the seat and covered his face with his hands. A tiny moan escaped from him.

"What is the matter?" cried Bobo.

"It is a murdered tree!"

There, indeed, was a problem. How far would they get with their hope of curing an elderly gnome of neurasthenia, if every time he saw a piece of wood he began to weep over a murdered tree? Rodney explained to him—it was not the gnomobile that had done the murdering. The poor innocent car could not help it. It was those wicked ones, the lumbermen who had done the evil thing. Glogo sat with his head in his hands, paying no heed. Elizabeth sat in the seat by Rodney, silent, not knowing how to help.

Rodney started the engine and backed out the gnomobile.

Soon they were speeding along the highway. This series of new events started Bobo exclaiming and healed Glogo's broken heart for a time. What was this spirit that was humming and purring underneath them and how did it make the gnomobile move? As Rodney had said, it was very obedient. It would take them exactly where they wished and at whatever rate of speed they decided on. Truly, it was a wonderful spirit!

But what was happening outside? The forest went flying past and Bobo and Glogo ran from the window on one side to the window on the other side. What was happening to the trees? The trees were running swiftly! They had never seen the trees behave this way before. Glogo held on to the wooden trim of the window, forgetting the dead trees in his amazement at the way the live ones were acting.

Very soon they came to a redwood grove which neither of them had ever before seen. They stopped. Once more Rodney wrapped his two charges in the robe and carried them into the forest.

When they were in a lonely place he put them on the ground and they went to work like bloodhounds to search for gnomes. They could find out quickly if there were any in this forest, so they told the big people, for gnomes have a keen sense of smell, and they leave traces of their breath on the ferns when they take the seed. They must cover a lot of ground in their search for food, fern seeds being very small. Rodney said he had read about Tibetan sheep, which have to feed on the run, because the clumps of grass which they eat are so far apart; and Bobo said it was almost that way with the gnomes.

They decided there were no gnomes in this forest, so they

49

were taken back to the gnomobile. The spirit of the sun carried them swiftly to another grove. Again they repeated the search and this went on all the rest of the day. They visited more forests than the oldest gnome in the world had ever dreamed of. They saw beautiful sights of nature; they saw squirrels and rabbits, and once a fox and once a deer— but no trace of gnomes.

It was interesting to see the squirrels come down from the trees and sit on a redwood stump and exchange greetings with Glogo. All the creatures of the forest were polite to gnomes, he explained, and came to them when they had wounds, because the gnomes knew how to gather the right plants and crush them to make poultices. Glogo and the squirrels could carry on a sort of talk, and they assured him there were no other members of their race near by.

When twilight began to add its shadows to the eternal dimness of the forest, they were in the grove which Rodney had purchased and given to the state, and which had his name on a bronze plaque at the entrance on the highway. But there were no gnomes here, and so they spread the robe on the floor once more and finished the remains of the food, and held a solemn talk.

"It is evident," said Rodney, "that there are no more gnomes among the coast redwoods, as these trees are called. But it is possible that we may find some among the true sequoias, which are up in the mountains. Do you know, Glogo, there are trees which grow to twice the size of those among which you live?"

Glogo did not know this and was greatly impressed that a big person should be able to tell him such news. "Where are these trees?" he asked, and Rodney told him they were in the interior of California, in the high Sierras. "We can go there tomorrow and see them, if you wish."

Glogo could wish nothing so much in the world. He said he would be deeply grateful to his new friend and to the spirit of the gnomobile if he could go there.

"There are problems in the way," said the young man. "You will be making a trip through places where men live and they have cut down all the trees and made farms where they grow their food. I am afraid seeing this will make you sad. Also, you will see many things which have been made out of murdered trees. Men have built themselves large wooden boxes in which they live. You will have to go into some of them—because, you see, Elizabeth and I must have some place to sleep, as we are not used to spending the night in the forest. You must make up your mind about all that before we set out."

Bobo, being young, was all excitement, desiring to see these new sights. What could be worse, he argued, than to live as they had, without any future? After all, Glogo knew that the trees had been murdered—he had imagined it and it could not be any worse actually to see it. What they wanted was to find gnomes. If there were bigger forests, with bigger trees, there might be whole tribes of their people in them.

So the old gnome bowed his head, and said he would endure whatever pain the ways of men might cause him. But he hoped he might be spared having to be seen by these men or to talk to them. Rodney said that he would get a couple of large wicker baskets which would have plenty of

The Gnomobile

holes for air. With pillows inside they would make perfect beds for gnomes. They could then be carried anywhere, and would not have to see any more than they wanted to see. Rodney said that the stores would still be open and if they hurried they might get the baskets.

They went back to the gnomobile, which took them with great speed out of the forest and into a town. This was, as Rodney had foretold, a painful experience for Glogo. In the fading light he saw hillsides from which every tree had been cut. They were so bare and desolate that he sighed with grief and could not look any more, but lay down upon the seat and went into a fit of melancholy. But Bobo, the youngster of only a century, was greatly excited by the new things. These wonderful big men had brought the very stars out of the sky and set them in their houses and along their highways. When they came to a town, he saw more bright stars than he had ever seen in the heavens and even Glogo had to sit up and ask questions about the spirits of these bright lights.

They parked the gnomobile on the street, with Glogo and Bobo safely hidden under the robe and the doors locked so that nothing could disturb them. Then Rodney and Elizabeth went into a hardware store and bought two lovely baskets with strong handles. In a "five-and-ten" they got two soft pillows and some big handkerchiefs to serve as sheets, as well as aluminum thimbles for drinking cups and some lovely soft tissue paper which Elisabeth could cut up for gnome handkerchiefs and napkins. She even found some doll's dresses, which she said were made-to-order nightgowns for her friends.

52

In Which the Gnomobile Sets Forth

In a drugstore they had the thermos bottles filled with hot and cold drinks. They took all these treasures back to the gnomobile. While Elizabeth sat and told the little people about them, Rodney went back to the drugstore and shut himself up in a telephone booth, and called Elizabeth's mother "long distance." He dropped several coins into the slot and said,

"Petunia, I called to tell you that we have had a lovely day and we have had a most fortunate meeting with a learned old gentleman. He is one of the greatest scholars in the state—Professor Glogo, head of the department of arboraceous psychology in Redwood University. He is traveling with his grandson, studying the history of the big trees, so it is very pleasant for Elizabeth and a cultural opportunity for both of us. I offered to take them to see the sequoias in the interior of the state and I hope you will let Elizabeth go along with me. I'll take the very best care of her."

Now, as it happened, Mama had received her education in a finishing school for young ladies and she had learned more about how to enter a drawing room than about scientific matters. She had never heard of Redwood University and she had no idea what arboraceous psychology might be—but nobody was going to get her to admit either fact. What she said was, "Oh, Rodney, you are such a fast driver!"

"I promise to drive very, very carefully, Petunia. We'll spend the night at a good hotel, one with a steel frame, so that it will not be shaken down by an earthquake. Also I will see that Elizabeth has her glass of milk at each meal."

"How long will you be gone, Rodney?"

"I'm not sure. It depends on the professor. What I think

is, we ought to learn all we can about the history of the largest trees in the world—just think, they are the oldest of all living things, Petunia, and Elizabeth is much interested in everything the professor tells her."

"I know, it's quite extraordinary how excited the child became about those trees. I suppose she wears the old gentleman out with questions. Don't let her get her feet wet, Rodney."

"I won't."

"What will she do about pajamas and a toothbrush?"

"We'll buy everything she needs, here in the town I am
phoning from. I'll call you again in a day or two and let
you know how we are."

So Mama said all right. Elizabeth went back into the store
and bought things for herself which she had entirely for-
gotten in her excitement over taking care of her wonderful
pair of pets. Rodney also provided for his needs and they
set out upon their journey south.

The wonderful gnomobile could travel just as well by
night as by day. It shot out sunshine before it so that one
could see the highway in front like a great ribbon of light.

55

It was a pretty thing when one was traveling in the mountains, winding this way and that, with the light playing among the trees. Bobo never grew tired of exclaiming about the spirit of the sun in the gnomobile and begged Elizabeth to hold him in her arms in the front seat in order that he might watch the spectacle.

On the other hand, Glogo, a sensible elderly gnome, declared that he had seen enough sights for the present, and laid himself down in his snug little basket-bed. Doubtless he had thoughts about the wickedness of men and the sorrows of gnomes, or perhaps he was learning to talk to the spirit of the engine. Anyhow, the others heard no more from him, and did not know what had been the effect on a gnome's neurasthenia of the first day of a change of scene.

At nine o'clock they came to a town, and Rodney declared that it was bedtime for both girls and gnomes. He stopped in front of a hotel which he said was safe against those earthquakes of which Mama stood in such dread. The gnomes were safely stowed in their baskets, along with their thimbles and nightgowns. When the bellboy came out from the hotel, Rodney would not let him touch these precious baskets, but told him to take the gnomobile to the garage.

Rodney entered the hotel lobby, a quite unusual figure with two large wicker baskets, followed by a little girl with paper bundles. He told the clerk that he wanted two rooms with connecting bath. The clerk looked at the baskets, and said, "I am sorry, sir, but we don't allow dogs in the rooms."

"I have no dogs," said Rodney.

"What is in the baskets, please?"

This was a difficulty which the guest had not foreseen and

he had to think quickly. "In the baskets are royal Abyssinian geese," he declared.

Elizabeth opened her mouth and gulped. And when the clerk also looked surprised, Rodney added that they were well-bred creatures, accustomed to living in homes of refinement, and would do no damage of any sort.

Elizabeth was uneasy. Suppose the clerk should look into the baskets and see Glogo and Bobo! How dreadful if Rodney should have to admit that he was telling a fib! Maybe the clerk would call the police and take them all to jail!

What he did was to ask Rodney to wait, please. He called the manager, who presently appeared and discussed the problem. He hinted some desire to inspect the geese, but Rodney told him that they were "confidential." In the end the matter was settled by Rodney's writing a paper in which he agreed that in consideration of being allowed to take a pair of royal Abyssinian geese into his room, he agreed to repay the manager for any damage they might do to the carpets or furniture. The manager had heard the name of Sinsabow, it appeared, and was content with this document.

They went into the elevator and were shown to their rooms. Rodney looked about carefully and told the bellboy to wait. He sat down at the desk and wrote a note to the management, calling their attention to the fact that there was a large spot on the carpet three feet from the northeast corner of the room, and also a spot on the cover of one of the beds, near the foot, at the right-hand side looking toward the foot. He handed this to the bellboy, then he took out his wallet and said, "Have a scantling."

The boy looked startled at the word, but apparently recognized what was put into his hand. He said, "Thank you, sir," and took himself away. Rodney locked the doors of the rooms and closed the transoms tight, after which Elizabeth opened the baskets. Up popped the two gnomes, wide-awake and full of curiosity about this new experience.

"What is a scantling?" demanded Bobo who, of course, had been listening to every word.

"It is the British word for a shilling," replied Rodney.

"Oh, Rodney, why do you play jokes on him?" cried Elizabeth. "It's just some of his foolishness, Bobo. A scantling is a piece of lumber, and Rodney is always making fun, because his money comes from lumber and he pretends that he gets mixed up about it. Excuse him, Bobo."

There was much lumber in these rooms, made into beds and dressers and desks and chairs. Glogo had been warned about it, but even so, he could not help being pained at the sight and he sat in his basket, a prey to sad thoughts. But Bobo was out and about, examining everything. Presently he was in the bathroom, with Elizabeth turning on the water in the tub and lifting him up, so he could see into the tub. He was kicking and squealing, calling to his grandfather to come and see this mountain spring in one of the big lumber boxes of the men.

Gnomes are very agile, it appeared—they could put their hands onto a chair and jump up to the seat. They could also clamber onto the bed by way of its legs. So presently the two little people were seated right up in the middle of one of the twin beds, asking questions.

"Why did you say we were geese?" asked Bobo.

"I hope you didn't object," Rodney replied. "From a certain point of view, you know, we are all of us geese."

"The goose is a worthy creature," said Glogo, "very digni-fied, and quiet unless you annoy her."

"What was the rest that you told him?" persisted Bobo.

"Abyssinian."

"What is that?"

"That is a country almost on the other side of the world. It is inhabited by very ancient people."

Elizabeth brought up another question. "Rodney," she said, "are you sure they *have* geese in that country?"

"By Jove, I never thought of it!"

Elizabeth was much troubled and Rodney, who was always ready to go along with a joke, said, "What can we do?"

"Don't you suppose the information may be in an encyclo-pedia?"

"It might. But the library will be closed now."

There they were, hopelessly stuck until a bright idea came to Rodney. "I'll have to cable to Abyssinia!"

"Oh! Won't that be expensive?"

"Maybe a dozen bundles of shingles—something like that."

"Rodney, do stop!" exclaimed Elizabeth. She had to ex-plain to the gnomes that shingles were sold in the lumber business and that Rodney was making more jokes about his money.

"But," said Rodney, "if it were not for the lumber business, poor Glogo would not have neurasthenia and you and I would not find ourselves in a hotel under false pretenses. I must really find out if they have geese in Abyssinia!"

He went to the telephone and called the telegraph office and told them to send a boy. Then he sat at the desk and began to write. Elizabeth had to explain to Bobo about cabling—

there was a wonderful spirit, so swift that it could travel many times around the earth in a second, and men had made a path across the bed of the ocean upon which it would travel.

In exchange for some of Rodney's money—or "lumber," as he put it—the spirit would take a message to this far-off country and bring back an answer. "It works while you sleep," added Rodney and explained that it was now morning in Abyssinia and the answer should be back by the time it was morning in California.

He read the cablegram, "United States Consul Addis Ababa Abyssinia do you have geese in your country Rodney Sinsabow."

The boy came and Elizabeth shut up the gnomes in the bathroom and then opened the door. The boy had never heard of Addis Ababa and had to telephone the office and wait while they looked it up. Finally he got the rate, including twenty words paid reply—there might be some important information they should have about Abyssinian geese, said Robney. He gave the boy a bill and said, "You may keep the change. It will be about one two-by-four fourteen."

The boy looked bewildered and made his escape quickly. Once more Elizabeth had to explain to the gnomes how lumber was cut and measured.

The gnomes in the bathroom dressed themselves in the doll's dresses, in which they looked most charming. They were made snug in their baskets, close by the open window, since they were particular about fresh air. Elizabeth poured some lemonade out of the thermos bottle into a glass and laid the thimbles alongside, so that they could dip some out. Gnomes drink frequently, it appears, having small stomachs.

They said that lemonade bore a very close resemblance to honeydew.

Then everybody went to sleep—or at any rate became quiet. If Glogo lay and nursed the age-old griefs of his race, the others did not know it. The evening breeze blew the curtains gently, and down on the street the electric signs winked yellow and red and blue all night. Bobo dreamed that he was courting a lively young lady at the foot of a giant sequoia. Elizabeth dreamed that she was attending a parliament of geese which were trying to make up their minds whether they were white or black and offered to pay her a dozen bundles of shingles if she would decide the question for them.

When the dawn crept up, the gnomes opened their eyes and snipped their honeydew and whispered softly to each other until the big people stopped their dreadful snoring. Rodney went to the telephone and asked for a cablegram, and there it was, brought by the swift spirit of electricity from Addis Ababa. Rodney read the message: "Yes we have all kinds of geese in Abyssinia as in California what kind are you Jones Consul."

"I might have known it," said Rodney. "They are all over the world."

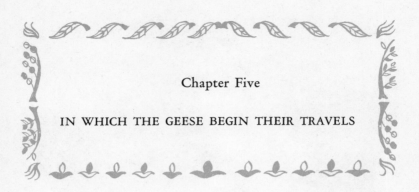

Chapter Five

IN WHICH THE GEESE BEGIN THEIR TRAVELS

Rodney telephoned orders for the gnomobile to be brought to the front of the hotel. The "royal Abyssinian geese" were packed safely, each in its own basket. Rodney carried the baskets downstairs into the lobby and waited while the management sent up to the rooms to make sure that no damage had been done to the carpets or furniture. Elizabeth stood by somewhat ill at ease, because all her life, when she had entered or departed from a hotel, her belongings had been in nice leather bags, carried by the bellboys, whereas now she had them in her arms, done up in paper bags.

She hoped nobody was paying any attention to them. But this was too much to hope for in California, where people take an interest in all things new and strange. A brisk young man was sitting in the lobby, and as soon as he spotted Rodney he came up to him. "Mr. Sinsabow?" he inquired.

"Er—yes," said Rodney, knowing right away the danger in which he stood.

"I understand you have a pair of geese in the baskets."

"Er—yes," said Rodney again.

"I am a reporter for the *Evening Whizzle-Bang*, our local newspaper. I wonder if you would be willing for me to see them."

"Sorry," said Rodney, "but they are strictly confidential."

"Why is that, may I ask?"

"Well, they are rare and valuable."

"But surely it wouldn't hurt for me to have a look."

"I'm afraid it would. You see, they are from Abyssinia, not Hollywood. They do not like publicity."

"But then, does no one ever see them?"

"No one but my niece and myself."

"You take care of them yourselves?"

"Quite so."

"You say they are royal Abyssinian geese? In what way do they differ from American geese?"

"Well, they are Abyssinian. That's quite different from American."

"Oh, yes, quite. But in just what way?"

"Oh, well, one might say they are royal. We do not have royalty in this country."

"Indeed! How interesting! May I ask if this means that they are especially intelligent?"

"Well, they know how to get into the baskets and out again and they tell us when they are hungry—"

"How do they tell you, Mr. Sinsabow?"

"They make sounds. It is really quite as if they spoke. As a matter of fact, they do speak. They speak Gnomic."

Elizabeth began to giggle and the young man looked at her resentfully, as if he thought she was laughing at him. So she got her face straight and said politely: "They are the only pair in the United States. At least, they are afraid they are."

"Indeed!" said the reporter. "I suppose they told you this in Gnomic. I realize that you and your uncle are making fun of me, but if you would allow their royal geese-highnesses to speak to me, they might give me a story without so many words."

To which Rodney solemnly replied: "They are greatly impressed with the California landscape; they think you have the most delightful climate in the world. You may say that in so many words."

"They prefer California to Abyssinia, then?" The reporter was writing briskly.

"Oh, very much. They don't see how anyone could wish

to return. They are impressed by your system of roads, of
which they have very few in their native country."

"Now we are going places! May I ask what royal Abyssinian geese look like?"

"Tell him about that, Elizabeth," said Rodney; and Elizabeth had to think in a hurry.

"I would say they are somewhat smaller than our American geese."

"What color are they?"

"They are pure white but they have a golden crown on
top of their heads and pink cheeks. They wear little brown
caps."

"How remarkable! Do they wear the caps over the crowns,
or vice versa?"

"I don't know what that last word means," said Elizabeth,
so Rodney answered for her, "It is a native custom."

"They were that way when you got them? I hope you
will tell me something about how you came—"

"No, no, I really cannot."

At this moment the management returned from its visit of
inspection and the rooms being in good order, Rodney was
permitted to pay his bill and escape. The young man from
the *Evening Whizzle-Bang* followed him through the lobby
and out to the gnomobile, praying for some hint as to why
the son of an American lumber magnate and his young niece
were unwilling to display the only pair of royal Abyssinian
geese in the United States. "Have you even been to Abyssinia, Mr. Sinsabow?"

"Have I, Elizabeth?" asked Rodney, unlocking the door
of the gnomobile.

"No," said Elizabeth, with decision.

"You are the son of Mr. Sinsabow, the lumberman of the Northwest, are you not?"

"Am I, Elizabeth?"

"He is one of his sons."

"And is your father interested in these geese?"

"My father doesn't know anything about them!" This from Rodney himself.

"Just an adventure of your own? May I ask, is it a business undertaking?"

"No, it is entirely in the interest of science. Get in, Elizabeth."

"Oh! You are conducting scientific experiments with these geese? May I ask—"

"I am truly sorry, but I cannot delay any longer."

"You can't possibly let me have just a peek, Mr. Sinsabow?"

"You must excuse me." And Rodney slammed the doors of the gnomobile, and took his seat and started the engine, and with a last polite smile at the reporter, backed out into the street and sped away.

Elizabeth reached down and unfastened the covers of the baskets, and out popped the younger gnome, bubbling over with questions. "What is a 'Whizzle-Bang'? What is a newspaper?" Elizabeth wanted to know if Mama would see the story. Rodney answered that when something absurd appeared in a paper some kind friend always sent you a clipping.

They were going down the Coast Highway—U.S. 101, the signs said. First there were hills covered with forests and lovely green streams in the valleys. Then it became warmer and there were fewer trees on the hills, and in the valleys fruit trees. The gnomes had never before heard of trees like that, tame trees which the big people made for their own use. Glogo was pessimistic about it, certain that such trees could come to no good end. He was not surprised to hear that they were subject to many diseases and had to be sprayed frequently with bad-smelling chemicals.

They came to the country which Jack London made famous as the Valley of the Moon. Rodney, who was as good as a guidebook, told them that Jack London was a famous writer who had loved the outdoors and all wild creatures. How he would have loved to meet gnomes and how eagerly he would have espoused their cause against the lumbermen!

Alas, Jack London had come to a sad end. The lovely estate on which he had dreamed of happiness had been cut up into tracts and the public was invited to buy romance at so much per front foot.

They shut the gnomes up in the baskets and stopped in a town and bought food. Rodney inquired for fern seed but it appeared there was none on the market. He got canary-bird seed, also caraway seed, which is used in making cakes. But it turned out that the gnomes did not care for these. They were getting along quite well on the big people's food, and already had begun to develop definite tastes.

They would not touch meat in any form—the idea of murdered animals was even worse than that of murdered trees, but they found ripe olives delightful things to nibble— "Just the right size," said Bobo. They craved something like the tiny shoots of plants which they sometimes ate, so Rodney guessed at a bunch of celery, which delighted them. So beautifully built was it that they were as much pleased with its shape as with its flavor. They liked to wrestle with it and pull off one stalk at a time; then they had something they could nibble at for hours.

They found a patch of woodland, not too close to the highway, and there they spread out the robe and had their lunch, safe from prying eyes. There Professor Glogo, head of the department of arboraceous psychology in Redwood University, gave them a most interesting lecture about the trees in this patch of woodland.

He talked with them and found them far from admirable. He lowered his voice as he told about them, explaining that it would do no good to hurt their feelings. They were smug and self-satisfied trees, content with the little narrow world which was all they knew. Utterly lacking in ideas of sublimity, they were satisfied to live for a bare fifty years or so, and the fate of being blown over by a storm and cut up for firewood did not trouble them. They had even come to the point where they ceased to be outraged by the idea of axes. They had never heard of gnomes, and most of the wild things of the forest were unknown to them. "They have lost their souls," said the professor of arboraceous psychology.

Elizabeth thought they were rather nice-looking trees but she knew it would not do to say so, and listened politely while her elders conversed on learned subjects. Glogo explained why it was that the murder of a forest was such a calamity for all the things of nature, even the big people. The forest was a device of the great Mother Nature to hold the soil, and the water in it, so that things could grow. The roots of the trees made a tangled mat, and held everything firm and safe. But once you cut off the trees and the roots died, then the soil was washed away, and the mountain slopes were stripped bare. In the end there would be no way to get anything to grow on that particular place.

Now, Rodney had the knowledge which he had got in the big people's university, and whenever the gnomes told him something that agreed with this teaching, he was surprised. "How strange that you should know that!" he would say.

Glogo would be surprised in turn. "We have had many, many years to watch nature," said he. "Do you suppose we have failed to notice how the water carries all things down? You can learn that by watching any trickle of water coming out of a mountainside with the tiny bit of earth it carries.

Always that goes down; never does it go up. If you pull the roots of the trees away, you will see a great deal of earth carried off—the water will be black with it. You can see it going until some other roots stop it and hold it. This goes on everywhere all the time, over the whole earth. Everything is carried down from the hills and there is nothing to take it back again."

All this was true, according to the best knowledge of men, said Rodney. But the trouble was that each man owned his little bit of land and did what he pleased with it and gave no thought to the harm he might do to other men, or to those who would come after him.

That was something Glogo had never heard about the big people and their affairs and he asked questions about the ways of men with the land. The more he heard, the more dreadful it seemed to him that one man should be allowed to keep land to himself.

"Never have we gnomes thought of such an idea. The forest belongs to us all, and anyone who did anything to harm it would be looked upon as a mad creature. What is the use of all your knowledge if you do not know how to save the means of life?"

Rodney was used to finding fault with the world in which he lived but somehow he did not like to have the gnomes do it. He tried to make excuses for the follies of men. They had grown that way—they had certain ideas and did not know how to change them. In fact, they would become angry with you if you tried to change them. The more Rodney explained this, the more Glogo suffered, and Elizabeth thought it was hardly the best way to cure a case of neurasthenia.

The only other way she could think of was to offer him a pickled onion.

The gnomobile got under way again. They were coming to the "bay district" and there were many towns with tame trees planted along the streets, but no more forests. Indeed, it seemed that the very memory of forests was gone from the world, and the heart of the old gnome became ever more depressed.

They came to the long bridge over Carquinez Strait. The gnomes had to pop down into their baskets because this was a toll bridge and if they were seen there would be a complicated problem as to how many gnomes it took to make one passenger. When danger was over they popped out again, marveling at the powers of the big people and at the courage of the gnomobile, which would venture out so high in the air over a deep river.

They came to a city, and then to another. It seemed to be one continuous city for many miles and there were more strange sights than ever before had assailed the eyes of gnomes. There were solid blocks of houses, some made of murdered trees, others of stone torn from the heart of the earth. The peace of the forest was replaced by tooting horns, ringing bells and cries of things for sale. Assuredly, the end of the labors of the big people was madness, said Glogo, and he lay down in his basket and closed his tired eyes.

As for Bobo, he raced from one side of the gnomobile to the other, crying out over this and that, like the child of a mere hundred years that he was. People saw his face at the window. Then the gnomobile raced on and they were left to wonder—had that been a doll or a monkey or a midget out of a circus?

Out of the city again, the highway went weaving through the hills, bare and smooth like human bodies. Already they were turning brown with the heat, and Glogo cried that it was because the trees had been cut and the hills had been washed into slopes like prostrate human forms as a warning to all murderers.

"I doubt if there ever were trees on these hills," said Rodney, "there isn't enough water." But Glogo asked if men could not bring water to the hills. Why was it that all their cunning went to destroying nature instead of to saving it?

They were now in the San Joaquin Valley, running almost straight for a hundred miles. It was all fruit orchards and vineyards and fields of one crop or another. There was no hope at all of finding gnomes there. It was getting hot, that dry baking heat which prunes and raisins require. Glogo was not used to it; the blazing sun burned his eyeballs and he moaned for the cool twilight of the redwoods.

Presently, the gnomobile stopped at a roadside stand and Elizabeth got out, having had a bright idea. When she came back, she had four little mountains of coolness, each held in its separate paper napkin, and the oldest of living Americans was invited to make the acquaintance of one of the newest of his country's inventions—the ice-cream cone.

Really, this was quite extraordinary, admitted Glogo, sitting up in his basket-bed and licking with his tiny tongue. What was this made of and by what magic was it turned to snow in the month of May? It tasted a little like the juices of

73

the aphis, but what made it such a pretty pink? And what made the little brown cup? And what made the stuff leak down the sides?

"That is because you don't eat it fast enough," explained Elizabeth. Glogo answered that this was not so easy if you were as little as a gnome and not used to being frozen up inside. As for Bobo, he was catching all the leaks before they started, and found it great fun. Each new invention of the big people seemed to him more delightful than the last.

The tireless gnomobile rolled into Fresno and they stopped to lay in supplies for supper. Rodney bought an evening paper, suggesting that there might be news of gnomes being discovered in some California forest. He did not find that, but a glance at the front page brought him back to the gnomobile, chuckling. He could hardly wait to get out of town to read the story to his passengers.

LUMBER SCION CARRIES PET GEESE

Only Royal Abyssinian Pair in America
Taken for Auto Tour

The brisk young reporter had seen the opportunity of a lifetime in that interview. He had gone back to the office and written up a gay fantasy on the subject of a young millionaire who had in some mysterious manner acquired a pair of royal Abyssinian geese and was taking them for an automobile tour for their health and education. The reporter hadn't had to exaggerate so very much. He had made them sacred geese as well as royal, giving them a direct lineage from that flock in the Roman temple which had saved the city by their cackling. He had made Rodney say not merely that they could indicate when they were hungry, but also that they could carry on a conversation. He had made Rodney say not merely that geese in Abyssinia wore peaked caps, but that they were hatched that way.

In short, the reporter had got all the fun from the brief interview that the liveliest fancy could concoct and his success was proved by the fact that his story had been carried by one of the press associations. This meant that it was appearing in hundreds of papers all over the country and was at that moment being enjoyed by millions of people.

First Rodney had to explain to Glogo and Bobo the magical devices of newspapers, whereby it was possible for a story told in northern California in the morning to be read in central California in the afternoon and perhaps on the other side of the earth on the previous afternoon. After that the "lumber scion" had a chance to reflect and at the next town he stopped and called in the aid of the magical spirit known as "long distance." He began dropping coins into a slot, and ringing deep-toned bells. Presently, he was saying, "Petunia, have you read the evening paper yet?"

"No, Rodney. What has happened?"

"There is a story about us in it."

"Oh, dear! Nothing bad, I hope!"

"Just a funny story. You see, the professor has collected a lot of valuable specimens. He is carrying them in a couple of baskets and he doesn't want any publicity about his work. When a reporter tried to find out from me what it was all about, I told him there were a pair of geese in the baskets."

"*Geese,* Rodney?"

"I said the first thing that came into my head and the reporter has had a lot of fun with it. It's no harm only I thought that my father mightn't understand, so please explain for me, will you, Petunia?"

"I will. How is Elizabeth?"

"She's right here."

So Elizabeth took the phone and said, "Oh, Mama, we're having such a lovely time. And we're seeing the prettiest country and I'm learning all about trees and forestry and conservation—you just can't imagine."

"Well, dear, Mama misses you terribly." Then she said, "All right, dear, go ahead and enjoy yourself, but don't fail to eat what you need and don't let yourself get caught out in thunderstorms, for you know how they frighten me."

Elizabeth wanted to say, "You won't be there, Mama." But being a wise little girl for her twelve years, she said, "All right, Mama, we'll be ever so careful. Good-by."

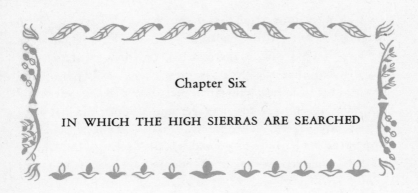

Chapter Six

IN WHICH THE HIGH SIERRAS ARE SEARCHED

The gnomobile was speeding south on the "inland route." There were no forests to be found anywhere here, so they waited until darkness had come, and then turned into a side road and found a place to spread their picnic supper. When another car came along, they saw the lights a long way off, and the two gnomes crawled under the robe and munched their celery stalks in darkness until the danger was past.

They drove on until bedtime, and stopped in a town as before. Rodney strode into the hotel lobby carrying his two baskets, followed by Elizabeth with their other belongings in a respectable suitcase which she had purchased. Rodney stated what rooms he wanted and wrote their names in the register. The clerk turned it about, read the name, and then broke into the kind of beaming smile which he reserved for leading statesmen and motion-picture actors.

"Mr. Rodney Sinsabow? Well, well, I'm delighted to meet you. Are these the royal Abyssinian geese?"

"Yes," said Rodney, with resignation.

"It is most interesting," said the clerk. "I have just been reading the story in the paper."

Fame has its drawbacks but also its conveniences. The story stated that the precious geese were well trained and never abused the hospitality of hotel rooms. So the clerk did not have to send for the manager and Rodney did not have to sign any papers. Quite the contrary—"We'll be delighted to put the bridal suite at your disposal, Mr. Sinsabow, and at no extra charge. We're much honored to have you as our guest."

They were taken upstairs to a pair of high-ceilinged rooms with beds having swans carved on them—"sorry they aren't geese," said the clerk, who had added himself to the bellboy as escort. The two stood around, unable to conceal their curiosity, until Rodney assured them that he and his niece were capable of opening the baskets themselves, and gave the bellboy a couple of "scantlings" to get rid of him.

Hardly had they pulled down the shades and closed the transoms and let the gnomes out of their hiding places, before the telephone rang and Rodney was saying: "No, I'm very sorry; please explain to the young man that I have been driving all day and cannot give any interviews tonight."

But this was not enough. The bell rang again and it was the young man himself. "Let me explain, Mr. Sinsabow. We have special orders from New York to follow up this story, wherever you can be found. You see, it's made a tremendous hit—the whole country wants to know more about the geese. I beg you to let me see them, Mr. Sinsabow, or at least tell me about them. I'll be ruined if I let this story get

by me. If you won't tell me anything, I'll simply have to make it up."

"Make up anything you please," said Rodney, with the magnificent recklessness of the rich.

He told the office not to ring the phone any more and hung out the "Do not disturb" sign on the doorknob. The gnomes went to sleep under the gentle ministration of an electric fan and Elizabeth, alone in her sumptuous chamber under another fan, dreamed that the royal Abyssinian geese had flown to their homeland.

Morning came—the hot dawn of the interior of California, promising a still hotter day and a crop of raisins which would break the market. Rodney looked outside the door of his room and discovered that the attentive management had placed a morning paper before every door. He took his copy and there was a story, set out by what is called a "banner headline," all the way across the front page:

ROYAL ABYSSINIAN GEESE IN TOWN

Lumber Scion Permits Inspection of Treasures

It appeared that the young reporter had taken Rodney at his word and made up anything he pleased—and how much he had pleased! He had pleased to tell how he had been admitted to the bridal suite of the hotel and had seen the royal Abyssinian geese in the bathtub—it appeared that they spent all their time swimming in the bathtub and slept that way, with their wings tucked under their arms.

The story became eloquent about the beautiful golden tufts on their heads, and the pink feathers on their cheeks. It told how charmingly they wagged their tails—on wag meant "I like you," two wags meant "I dislike you," and three quick wags meant "Go to the devil."

The handsome and charming young scion of the lumber family still refused to tell how he had come into possession of these valuable creatures. He was collecting their eggs, one of which was laid under the bed every morning. His niece was carrying them in a suitcase and when there were thirteen, which was the royal mystic number in Abyssinia, the mother goose would set on them. Meanwhile she was seeing California and expressed, in Gnomic, her great delight with the raisin and prune country. Rodney had explained that she would speak words only under the influence of bright sunshine; all the way down the San Joaquin Valley she had been chatting gaily.

The phone rang and it was the young reporter on the wire, wanting to know if his story was O.K. Rodney said it was the best piece of scientific exposition he had ever read in an American newspaper. The reporter asked where Rodney was going with his treasures and Rodney told him to make that up, also. The reporter wanted to know if he could have a photograph, and Rodney said, "Use one of the Governor," and hung up.

They ordered a breakfast of coffee and toast and marmalade for Rodney, milk and orange juice and cereal for Elizabeth—just what Mama would approve. While the gnomes were breaking off bits of toast and dipping them into marmalade, the phone rang again and it was a reporter from another press association, saying that San Francisco headquarters had wired him to send more details. Rodney said he was very sorry, he had none with him, and hung up and told the hotel not to ring again. A few minutes later there was a tap at the door—a humble note from the reporter, begging at least to know what the royal Abyssinian geese ate. Rodney wrote underneath, "Breakfast, marmalade and toast; dinner and supper, celery and ice-cream cones."

They packed up and ventured down into the lobby, where quite a crowd was waiting to see them, including three active young men with large black boxes. They begged frantically for just one "shot" of the geese, and Rodney let Elizabeth pay the hotel bill, while he kept his hands on the baskets lest these too eager fellows should try to snatch them away. They wanted Rodney and Elizabeth to line up and be photographed —just as if they were motion-picture magnates or diplomats arriving from Europe. Rodney would not pose, so they were snapped walking through the lobby and getting into the gnomobile in the street. This drew still more of a crowd— you'd have thought the circus had come to town.

As soon as the gnomobile had started down the street, Bobo wanted to get out of his basket and ask about cameras and photographers, but Rodney said no, he must wait. He was driving on the main street and Elizabeth asked, "Aren't you going the wrong way?" He answered that he thought they were being followed and presently he was driving fast here and there through the town, swinging around corners at a rate which caused discomfort to the gnomes. He was watching in his rear-view mirror. Elizabeth turned and watched through it too and sure enough, there was a car with two men in it following them. Every time they went around a block the other car went around the same block.

Rodney kept on crossing the main street at places where there were traffic signals. Finally he had a chance to dash across in front of a signal as it was changing and the crossing was blocked by other cars. The carload of reporters had to wait. Rodney went on at high speed and turned several corners until he was sure the pursuers were lost. Then the gnomes were let out and Rodney explained to them the mysteries of newspaper photography and also of traffic signals.

They began climbing into the foothills, bound for the Sierra National Park. There were trees again, real trees, worthy of the attention of a thousand-year-old gnome.

Glogo stood up and began to take an interest. The highway wound its smooth way up, up into the mountain passes. Glogo would point to this tree and that, heroes of bygone ages. He would read the stories of their centuries-long battles with the elements and interpret their souls. Such trees were tense and grim, never relaxing for a moment their labors to seek material and build defenses against coming storms. No rest or security in the mountains!

Down below were streams of clear cold water, such as you had when you let the forests remain as nature had planned them. How many things a gnome could tell about what went on in these gorges and in beautiful mountain meadows surrounded by forests—how the trees felt and what the flowers and grasses said to one another in their own language! Glogo became, in fact, the professor of arboraceous psychology.

The gnomobile rolled into the first grove of the sequoias. They stood, old monsters of the days before Glogo's great-grandfather, many of them thirty feet across—and not where the base spread out, but above the base. They were not so tall as the redwoods, but sturdier—in truth, real mountains of wood. In the days of the pterodactyls and dinosaurs, such trees had covered the whole northwest of the American continent. Now there were only a few thousand of them left, set aside in national parks. Their sap was poisonous to insects and other pests. They were safe from storms because their branches were brittle and could be blown off and replaced in the course of the centuries.

Their only danger was fire. You could read on the trunks of most of these giants the story of their struggle with the dread enemy of forests. Their bark was iron-hard, difficult to burn, but the underbrush would flame about them and eat holes in their bases. Then their sap would boil and ruin the heart of the tree. Still the mighty trunk would stand, hollow inside, but sending up its sap under the bark and nourishing its branches high up under the sky. You could see a crippled wreck with one line of bark, no more than a foot wide, running up to the top, feeding one feeble branch, a last gasp of tree-life.

The highway had been built to spare the trees. It twisted past this one and that, sometimes shaving off the edge of the roots. You could put out your hand and touch the monster as you passed. Once the road went right through a fire-scarred tree, and that was a sight that every tourist went home to tell about. There was plenty of room for the gnomobile and for a whole company of gnomes as well—but they were not there. It was hard to see where they could be in the groves, for the underbrush had been cleared away to remove the danger of fire. The sequoias do not grow out of dead stumps like the redwoods. Each baby tree has to start from a seed and the seed cannot grow in the debris which has carpeted the forest floor from the beginning of sequoia time.

It was a lovely journey, with no end of fascinating sights, but alas! no gnomes. They drove through grove after grove on the main highway and on roads less traveled. They would get out and Rodney would carry the baskets back into the forest and there release his friends. They would make their search but never with any result.

Rodney talked with one of the foresters, asking about other groves and meadows away from the traveled paths. They spent the whole day visiting such places and the heart of Glogo sank lower and lower. When twilight was falling, and they sat in a quiet nook eating their supper, he said there was no use to do any more—there were no gnomes in the sequoia forest. He lost all interest in lemonade and celery, bread and cheese, ripe olives and pickled onions, and fell into such a deep pit of neurasthenia that it was a hard labor to drag him out again.

"It is really foolish to give up hope, Glogo," argued Rodney. "America is a vast continent and many parts of it are covered with forests. Take these Sierras—they extend for hundreds of miles, and are covered with trees on both slopes. We might find gnomes in any of them."

But the patriarch of the gnomes was not comforted. All his people had always lived among the big trees. If they found gnomes in other forests, they would be different—they might not even speak the same language.

"Bobo and I could teach them!" cried Elizabeth. "That would be fun, wouldn't it?"

Bobo agreed to this promptly. He would be willing to marry a nice lady gnome even if she talked Siwash—a language which his forefathers had heard among the Indians.

"But even if we found them," persisted Glogo, "they would be at the mercy of the big people, who have mastered the whole earth and made everything different. What place could there be for gnomes in your cities—unless it were for newspapers to tell stories about?"

"I am sure it would be easy to find some useful things for them to do," said the optimistic lumber scion. "I would ask my father to set aside a reservation for gnomes. You could

have visitors' day once a week or something like that, and
the rest of the time you would be let entirely alone."

"We do not want to be dependent upon any man's charity," declared Glogo coldly. "We gnomes have always been
independent. But now you see how we have to impose upon
your kindness, to have your gnomobile take us about—"

"Oh, dear," cried Rodney. "Please do not think such things
as that. It has been the greatest pleasure I have ever had."

"It's been a lovely holiday!" broke in Elizabeth. "Rodney
was just sitting around the house, reading books and not
knowing what to do with himself."

"Just so, Glogo. I was so bored I was about to develop a case of neurasthenia too."

It occurred to Rodney that the best way to get the old fellow out of his troubles was to tell him somebody else's. So Rodney began to draw a picture of the plight of a lumber scion, destined to inherit a fortune some day and having that thought always in his mind.

"You see, my friend, there is nothing I can do at home. There are servants whose duty it is to do it for me, and if I should attempt to do it I should be getting in the servant's way and he would resent it."

"What a very strange situation!" said the old gnome, beginning to be interested.

"It has been that way ever since I was a baby—there was somebody to do everything and I wasn't allowed to do it."

"It is hard for a gnome to understand anything like that," said the thousand-year-old one. "Each of us has always had to stand on his own feet and do everything for himself."

"Well," said Rodney, "if you will let me take you on a tour, I can feel that I am helping science and I'll enjoy it far more than playing golf or writing verses which nobody will read."

"That is certainly most kind," said Glogo. "No person, whether big or little, could go farther in trying to make another person happy." So, without much hope of success, but in order to meet his friend halfway, Glogo would accept the invitation. Also, he would do his best to stop having the blues and be as good company as he knew how.

So there were the two of them, bowing to each other as politely as a couple of Japanese. Presently they were studying a map and making plans for a visit to Yosemite to see what kind of gnomes might dwell in those forests.

Chapter Seven

IN WHICH THE GEESE VISIT A BEAUTY PARLOR

They drove back to the highway. At a new town, Rodney stopped and bought an afternoon paper. There on the front page was the story of their morning's adventure, with the queer food habits of the royal Abyssinian geese. There was a picture of Rodney with his head bowed and one of Elizabeth making a face and one of the Governor. There was even an account of the chase of the gnomobile, with a record of the speed at which Rodney had driven—a truly terrible thing for Mama to be reading! There was a description of the vehicle and its license number. Said Rodney: "They'll be offering a reward for us next."

"What'll we do?" asked Elizabeth, who couldn't help being thrilled by the chase and the picture of herself in the paper. Rodney answered that they would have to travel "incog." He explained that visiting royalty, desiring to avoid social duties, would often take some other name. If that was all right for kings and princes, it would surely be all right for lumber scions.

Rodney said that from then on he was Mr. Jeremiah Titherton Jenkins of Kalamazoo, Michigan. Elizabeth thought that was a funny name and wondered how Rodney ever thought of it. Rodney said you had to choose a funny name or it might turn out to be the name of a real person and the person might be a check forger or wanted for holding up a bank.

Elizabeth giggled with excitement. "And what will I be?" she asked. "Do girls hold up banks?" Rodney said there were robberesses but she had better be his daughter or she might be his governess, as she preferred. What was her name to be? Elizabeth answered that she had wished her name was Jacqueline Kennedy but Rodney did not think that would help them avoid newspaper reporters.

Finally they agreed that Lucita Louise Jenkins was a nice, musical name, not apt to belong to a check forger or robberess. Bobo decided that he, too, ought to travel "incog." Among the giant sequoias they had seen one named "General Sherman," so Bobo would be General Sherman until he thought of some better name.

But they could not get Glogo interested in assuming the name of some big person. Nor did he like having Bobo bear the name of any big person, even a general. It was plain that Glogo didn't want Bobo to be too much interested in the affairs of the big people.

Bedtime came and they stopped in a town. They did not take the gnomobile to a hotel, but parked it in a garage. The man in charge had apparently not read the afternoon papers and handed them their check without comment or inquiry. Rodney took the two baskets and Elizabeth the suitcase and they trudged around the corner to a hotel. Rodney went to the desk and wrote, "Jeremiah Titherton Jenkins, Kalamazoo,

Mich.," and "Lucita Louise Jenkins, ditto, ditto," and made his usual request for two rooms with connecting bath.

The clerk looked at the two baskets, and said, "Pardon me, sir, but we do not allow pets in the rooms."

"I have no pets," said Rodney. "The baskets contain anthropological specimens."

"I see," said the clerk, but looked as if he did not see altogether clearly. However, he told the bellboy to take them up to 317 and 319. Rodney was serious and dignified and said nothing about giving away any scantlings. They locked the doors and made themselves comfortable and there was no ringing of the telephone or rapping on the door. They all slept peacefully—Elizabeth dreaming that she was Jacqueline Kennedy making a triumphant state visit to Addis Ababa, Abyssinia.

Next morning everything remained quiet and when they went down into the lobby there were no reporters or photographers. "Good morning, Mr. Jenkins," said the polite clerk. "I hope you rested well." Rodney said they had and paid the bill and resisted efforts of the bellboy to carry the baskets or to go to the garage and get his car. They went out onto the street alone. Rodney sighed with relief and said: "I think I'll be Mr. Jenkins for the rest of my life."

They got into the gnomobile and Rodney drove to a repair shop, having thought out a plan to make his little charges more comfortable. For one thing, the rear seat of the car was not high enough for them to see out of the windows without standing on something. For another, when the car passed over a bump, they were apt to be shot up to the ceiling, and when it stopped suddenly they would be tumbled off the seat. So

91

Rodney wanted an extra cushion put on top of the seat and he wanted to have some rings screwed into the woodwork and a couple of ropes across the front of the seat, for the gnomes to hold onto.

Rodney stopped in front of the repair shop and the man came out. Rodney told what he wanted but, of course, not explaining why. The man said that he could find a cushion that would fit well enough but it mightn't match the upholstery. Rodney answered that that wouldn't matter, they would put a cover over it. A workman came to screw the rings in place and Rodney took the baskets and set them on the front seat. Maybe he was too careful in handling them. Anyhow, there came a look in the workman's eyes—that peculiar light which to royalty traveling "incog" conveys the dread fact that it has been recognized.

The workman went inside to get some tool and of course he told others what he had discovered. Presently there was a stenographer standing at the window and several other employees with nothing to do but gape at the lumber scion and his niece, and the car which had the royal Abyssinian geese in two baskets on the front seat, and was having the rear seat raised so that the geese could look at the scenery, and ropes put across so they would not fall off. Could you imagine anything crazier?

Of course, a passerby stopped to see what it was all about, and then another, and another. The magic word began to spread up and down the street, "It's the geese! The Abyssinian geese!"—and people were running out of the stores and across the street and there was a crowd as if it were a fire or a holdup.

Rodney and Elizabeth were caught. There was no place

for them to take the baskets. If they had, the crowd would have followed them. They had to stand there and give their attention to the fitting of the extra seat and the proper placing of the rings, and try to look as if there were not half a dozen boys peering into their faces and into the front windows of their car.

And finally came the ultimate calamity—a brisk young man elbowing his way through the crowd. "Good morning, Mr. Sinsabow, I am a reporter for the *Evening Fizzle-Toot,* our local newspaper. We are very, very happy to have you in our town."

"As you can imagine, I'll be very, very happy to get out of your town," said Rodney grimly.

"You're having alterations made in your car? For the convenience of the geese, no doubt?" The young man was as excited as if he had just discovered gold in California. "May I ask just what are the alterations? An extra seat? That is to raise the geese up, I presume. Aren't their necks long enough?"

"Their necks are not as long as those of the people who are trying to see them."

"Please, Mr. Sinsabow, I beg you to excuse me for intruding. We reporters can't help it. We're given a certain assignment—and we have to live, you know."

"As a famous man once said, 'Sir, I fail to see the necessity.'"

But the reporter was not to be stopped. "You are having ropes put across? That, I assume, is to keep them from being hurt. They haven't been hurt, have they? Please tell me, have they been hurt?"

"They were quite well when I last saw them."

"They're in the baskets, aren't they? May I have just a look, so I can say I saw them?"

"You will say you saw them anyhow, so what is the difference?"

"I see you don't like reporters, Mr. Sinsabow—"

"There is a story of a man who was thrown out of a restaurant three times, and at last he sat up and said, 'I know what is the matter. They don't want me in there.' "

"Mr. Sinsabow, there is one question that has never been covered in any of the stories I have read about your geese and that is, their names. They have names, haven't they?"

"Oh, yes."

"May I ask what they are?"

"The gander is named Jeremiah Titherton Jenkins and the lady goose is named Lucita Louise Jenkins."

Elizabeth giggled and bit her lip to keep from giggling more. The reporter had a bunch of copy paper in his hand and was writing furiously. He repeated the names, "Jeremiah Titherton Jenkins" and "Lucita Louise Jenkins," as he wrote. Then he added, "Those are not Abyssinian names, surely?"

"Oh, no," said Rodney, "they are translations."

"And what are the original Abyssinian names?"

"Jacqueline Kennedy and General Sherman."

"You are kidding me," said the reporter.

"Oh, surely not!" replied the other.

Discussion was cut short by another man who came pushing through the crowd, carrying one of the dreaded black boxes. "Stand back, please," he begged the crowd. "I want to get a photograph."

"Oh, please don't stand back!" exclaimed Rodney.

The cameraman, digging his way back into the crowd, pleading and shouting, was getting room and holding his camera ready. Rodney, in desperation, laid hold of a fat man who stood close to him, and shoved him in front. "You take my place," said he.

"But I don't want him! I want *you!*" cried the cameraman.

"But *I* want *him!*" insisted Rodney.

The cameraman pleaded with the fat man to get out of the way, but Rodney whispered into the fat man's ear, "I'll pay you twenty-five dollars if you'll keep in the way." The fat man stayed in the way.

Elizabeth had started to be frightened of all this crowding and shouting. But she saw that Rodney was shaking with laughter, so she began to laugh also. The workman had stopped working and didn't seem to have any idea of starting again. The extra seat had been put in and Rodney decided to let that suffice.

Still keeping the fat man as a shield, he told the workman to leave the rings and the screws in the car, paid the agreed price and the fat man, and told Elizabeth to jump in. He took the basket out of his seat and handed it to Elizabeth and tooted the horn for the crowd to get out of the way. So the gnomobile got going and crawled down the street, with a string of half a dozen cars following. It took quite a while to shake them off and get to a peaceful place where they could let the gnomes out of hiding.

What was it? What had happened? Bobo had a hundred questions. How provoking to be shut up in the dark all that time! Elizabeth explained about the fat man and the angry photographer. Bobo was coming to understand the social importance of his friends, and to be as much interested in this as any reader of the tabloids. Perhaps he would have been willing to come out of his basket and have his picture taken, and published with theirs in all the newspapers of the world!

But not so Glogo. The thousand-year-old one listened in a silence which was a sort of rebuke. An uproar such as he had just heard confirmed his idea that the world of men was really mad. He had come to realize by now that the big people were powerful and controlled the fate of all gnomes. As a neurasthenia cure, the journey of the gnomobile was not proving a success.

Rodney guessed as much. "I'm beginning to think the Abyssinian goose story is played out," said he. "We shall have to get rid of those geese."

"But how?" cried Elizabeth.

"Well, we could kill and eat them—"

"Oh, Rodney!"

"Or we could give them away or sell them for the benefit of charity."

"But we haven't *got* them, Rodney!"

"Well, we'll have to get them. The world won't let us alone till we do."

"Let's go to Abyssinia!" piped up Bobo.

But Rodney said he didn't think this was possible. What they had to do was to find some Abyssinian geese in California. They would have to postpone the gnome hunt and set out on a tame-goose chase. Glogo would approve of that —he would like geese better than he did people.

In Which the Geese Visit a Beauty Parlor

Rodney stopped in the first town, and went into a hardware store, and bought two covered baskets, even bigger than the ones they had been using. In a "five-and-ten" he bought a set of child's water-color paints and some brown cloth, needles and thread. "Now we're ready for the goose chase," said he. He asked Elizabeth to sew two little caps, the size of those worn by Glogo and Bobo, with little straps underneath to hold them on the heads of the geese.

It would be hard to find geese in the San Joaquin Valley, there being no lakes or streams, and the water being pumped up from underground. Rodney took the road through one of the passes leading to the coast. It was a beautiful drive and before long there were forests, enough to make it worth while for them to look for gnomes. Coming down into a valley, there were farms and behind one of the farmhouses a glimpse of a pond and on it—glory hallelujah!—snow-white geese.

Rodney parked the gnomobile a distance from the house, not wanting to chance having it recognized. Carrying the new baskets, he went in and talked with the farmer and learned that a young and lively pair of geese could be had for four dollars. He paid the money and the farmer got some grain and called the birds to a feast.

He chose a gander and Rodney chose a goose and they fell upon them—and what would not Bobo and Elizabeth have given to witness that battle! Impossible to have imagined the strength of wing and leg and neck possessed by a young and lively California goose and the amount of pushing it took to get her into a basket and fasten the cover down. Before the battle was over Rodney's face was red, his well-tailored suit

97

was in need of brushing, and there was a scratch on his hand which might have been made by a beak and might have been made by a claw—Rodney could not have told which.

He carried his prizes back to the gnomobile, and you may believe there was a full load of baskets and suitcases and geese and gnomes and girl! When they found a safe, quiet place for their lunch hour, Rodney set the baskets of geese on the ground and told Elizabeth to get the water-color paints ready, wetting the little square of orange paint and the little square of pink paint. Every child knows you have to work at these paints a while to get a lot of them dissolved. Elizabeth worked, while Bobo asked questions about paint—what

flowers did it come from, and was it good to eat? At last Elizabeth said they were ready and Rodney took his seat on top of one of the baskets and lifted the cover enough to permit a goose's head and neck to be thrust out.

A young and lively goose is quiet while it is in the dark, but not so when it has a hope of freedom. Rodney had to sit tight and take a firm grip with one hand on the neck and with the other hand on the bill. "Goosie," said Elizabeth, "don't you know this is a beauty parlor? Talk to her, Bobo, and explain." But Bobo, unfortunately, did not know what a beauty parlor was, and did not know how to translate it into Goosic. He could understand a few words of wild-goose talk but these barnyard creatures were strangers to him.

Elizabeth took her paintbrush and with the loving care of a born artist put a delicate pink tinge upon the cheeks of each of the geese. "All the ladies do it," said Rodney. "So why shouldn't the other geese do it?"

Elizabeth added a delicate golden ring on top of their heads, just outside of where the caps would fit. She tried the caps on and they were perfect. She wanted to leave them on but Rodney said no, the geese might knock them off into the baskets and eat them or sit on them—who could say? The caps were to be for state occasions. So the necks and heads of the geese were shoved back into the baskets, and Rodney said, "I think it would be nice to have a poem about our geese, don't you?"

"Oh, yes!" cried Elizabeth and Bobo in chorus. They sat gazing in awe while Rodney thought for a few minutes. At last he recited,

> We are the Abyssinian geese,
> We prove that wonders never cease;
> We're hatched with golden crowns in sight,
> Saving the coronation rite;
> Already painted for the ball
> We need cosmetics not at all;
> And when our tails have agitations
> Reporters gather from all nations.

After that they had lunch. Then Rodney got out his pen and a writing pad and wrote some telegrams which he read to gnomes, geese and girl.

"Manager Imperial Hotel San Francisco: Reserve suite for press conference with royal Abyssinian geese at five this afternoon. Rodney Sinsabow."

That was number one. The second was to all newspapers and press associations in the big city.

"The royal Abyssinian geese, otherwise known as Jacqueline

Kennedy and General Sherman, invite you to a reception in their suite at the Imperial Hotel this afternoon at five."

Also one to the secretary of the Green Cross, which Rodney explained was a society devoted to forest preservation. Glogo would approve of that, said Rodney, and excuse all this foolishness if it helped to save the homeland of the gnomes. Glogo stood up in his basket and thanked Rodney very politely, after which Rodney read the telegram.

"I desire to present the royal Abyssinian geese to your society, to be sold at public auction for the furtherance of your work. Please have representative at press conference Imperial Hotel this afternoon at five."

There was one more telegram, addressed to an auctioneer whose name Rodney got out of a San Francisco newspaper. He also was invited to attend the conference and Rodney said he would be sure to come because auctioneers live by publicity. Fame in the affairs of big people meant money, so he explained. And money was something which most big people wanted very much. Glogo sighed and went back to his basket and had a bad fit of neurasthenia.

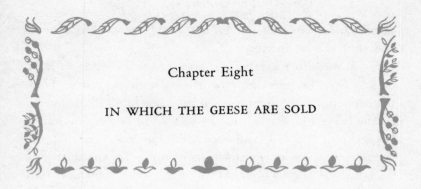

Chapter Eight

IN WHICH THE GEESE ARE SOLD

The gnomobile was loaded up again and they drove at high speed to the coast. At the first town Rodney got out and filed all his telegrams. The spirit of the lightning would take them at once to the great city and all the persons who had been invited would come at the appointed hour. Later, at another town, Rodney got the afternoon papers and there was a story of their morning adventures—how they had registered at a hotel under the name of Jenkins, and how they had had their car fixed for the convenience of the geese, and how the eccentric young lumber scion had hired a fat man to stand between him and a camera. After Rodney had read all that, he was more than ever sure there would be plenty of guests at his "press conference."

Rodney timed his driving so that they drew near the Imperial Hotel just a few minutes before the hour. He apologized to the gnomes because they would have to miss this show. He apologized to Elizabeth, also, because he thought she ought to stay with the gnomes to keep them safe. Rodney would get through and return as quickly as possible. Then they would all be free and get out of the crowded, noisy city and back to the forests.

He drove into a garage, and arranged to park for an hour or so. Then he took the two baskets with the geese. How the bellhops came hopping when they saw him! This time he let the baskets be carried, for he wanted to be very dignified. He went to the desk and registered and was told that the "conference" was waiting. He tried to pay for the suite, but the hotel was pleased to donate it. The management gave him to understand that any time he had a story like this he would be welcome. Rodney went upstairs, followed by two bell-hops with the baskets, and there was a big room with a score of men in it—reporters, photographers, the secretary of the Green Cross and the auctioneer—all waiting for the lumber scion who was the center of the world's spotlight just then.

Rodney was the soul of politeness. No more flippancy, no more hiding behind fat men! He made a little speech, with the reporters scribbling busily on their wads of copy paper.

"Gentlemen: For some time I have been conducting what I thought was a worthwhile scientific experiment. It was necessary that this experiment be carried on quietly; but unfortunately the news of it leaked out. It happened because the management of a hotel insisted upon knowing what I had in my baskets. When I said they were geese, they apparently thought it was good business to tell a newspaperman. Since that time I have been followed about and besieged by crowds and the things I wanted to do have become impossible. This publicity has naturally been intensely disagreeable to my family. You know what happened to my niece and me this morning and I have to find a way to stop it."

In Which the Geese Are Sold

The reporters nodded their heads. They, the makers of publicity, understood that many people pretended not to like it and that a few very rich ones really didn't. When this actually happened, it was most impressive.

"For some time," continued Rodney, "I have been interested in the work of the Green Cross, a society which is working for the preservation of our forests and our soil. I realize that these geese may be worth a great deal of money on account of the interest of the public, so I have decided to donate them to the Green Cross, to be sold at public auction for the benefit of its work. I have asked the secretary to come here, and I hope he will be willing to accept the gift."

The secretary was introduced and the reporters, who had never heard of the Green Cross before, asked many questions and made notes of the answers. It was a grand "boost." The secretary told the world that the society would be delighted to receive the geese and thanked Mr. Sinsabow with the greatest cordiality.

Then it was the turn of the auctioneer. Rodney said he had invited this gentleman because of his professional experience and hoped that he would be willing to take charge of the sale of the geese. The auctioneer said that he, too, was deeply interested in the work of the Green Cross and would perform the service without charge. "I imagine there won't be much expense for advertising," said he, and the reporters grinned.

One thing more, the exhibition of the geese, and the photographing. "You gentlemen of the press may have wondered as to my making a secret of the geese," explained Rodney. "They are half wild and easily frightened. They are not used to strangers and it upsets them and interferes with their training. Of course, I am now giving up trying to train them. They belong to the Green Cross, which assumes the responsibility; you may see them and take pictures of them— but you must not expect me to show you what they have learned. Maybe somebody else may be able to persuade them to speak and act in company. I have never been able to and I have never claimed to, and that is that. I'll take them into the other room and let them out of the baskets—they are always rather violent when they first come out. I'll do my best to quiet them, but I can't make any promises as to what they'll do."

Rodney was so impressive about it, you would have thought he was going to release a pair of royal Bengal tigers in a suite

of the Imperial Hotel. He bade the bellboys carry the baskets into the adjoining room. After the boys had retired, he locked the door, and sitting on top of one basket, he let the goose get its head out, and fitted on the little brown cap, and stepped back and let the creature climb out.

Rodney had no idea whether the goose would try to knock the cap off, or whether she would rush at him, or crawl under the bed, or what. He had a few grains of corn in his pocket and scattered these on the floor in the hope that the goose would not be too much of a goose—and this hope was justified, for the creature went right to work eating. The other one was let out in the same way. When they had eaten up all the corn, they backed into a corner and Rodney went quickly to the door and opened it, and said, "Come in, gentlemen."

The company entered. There was an actual pair of geese and they did actually have pink cheeks and a golden ring around their heads and little peaked caps on top. There they stood, looking frightened and wild enough. It wasn't much of a spectacle but, such as it was, the whole world was waiting for it and the photographers went right to work. The bulbs began to flash. Presently they were "shooting" Rodney standing near the geese, and the secretary of the Green Cross, and even the auctioneer. The first photos of royal Abyssinian geese ever taken in America!

Of course, the reporters wanted to ask more questions, but Rodney cut them short. "Gentlemen, I have told you the story. I am not a showman and I am not going to try to get these frightened creatures to perform in a hotel room. I have done all I can for you, and the next show is the auction."

"When will that be?"

"That is up to the new owners of the geese. If I may suggest, it would be wise to wait three or four days, so that those who are interested in the sale may have notice. Is that not so?" asked Rodney of the auctioneer. The man agreed.

"One question more, Mr. Sinsabow," broke in one of the reporters. "I understand you have some eggs."

"Yes, we have thirteen eggs."

"And what do you intend to do with them?"

Poor Rodney! His mind was quick, but not quick enough in that emergency. "We're going to put them into an incubator," said he.

He saw his mistake the moment the reporter spoke again. "Oh, then you'll have some royal Abyssinian goslings!"

"Yes, I suppose so."

"And how long do they take to hatch?"

"About three weeks, I suppose."

"And where will you be then?"

"I don't know about that."

"Are you going to take the incubator in your car?"

"Oh, no, no, no!" exclaimed Rodney, getting into a panic. "I have made arrangements for a well-known goose hatchery to take care of the eggs."

"And will you let us know what happens?"

"Yes, of course. We'll have another conference. And in the meantime these gentlemen"—he indicated the secretary and the auctioneer—"will make arrangements for the auctioning."

With that the lumber scion bowed himself out of the room and made his escape by a side door of the hotel. After he had walked for a distance to make sure he was not being followed, he hurried to the garage, where Elizabeth sat patiently waiting with her gnomes.

"Let me out! Let me out!" Bobo was squealing; and Glogo was commanding: "Be still, boy, be still!" There was almost an insurrection in the gnome family because of Bobo's excitement about that "press conference." He could hardly wait till the gnomobile was out of the garage and Elizabeth was free to take the top off the basket. "Did the reporters come?" and "How did the geese behave?" and "Did the paint look all right?"

"I think we'll have three weeks of peace now," said Rodnew. "Nobody's interested in eggs until they are ready to hatch."

But all the same, after thinking it over he said it would be better for them to remain "incog." They must choose some new names. Elizabeth was delighted—it was like playing a game. Rodney said that he would be Mr. Timotheus T. Pettigrew, of Oshkosh, Wisconsin. Elizabeth took a long time about her name, but finally decided on Pamela Pettigrew. Bobo had recently learned that the sequoias had been named for an Indian, so he would be an Indian of that name. Glogo wasn't interested in such foolishness, but Elizabeth and Bobo decided to name him after the General Grant tree in the Sequoia National Park.

They had to decide what to say was their new occupation. Rodney suggested that they should be collecting specimens of the different kinds of ferns. They could really collect some, and have them sticking out of the baskets, and so they would be telling the truth. They would be botanists. Right away they began to act the part. Elizabeth wanted to know how many kinds of ferns there were and asked Glogo to tell them about his conversations with these ancient plants in the redwood forests.

They left the noisy city and crossed a long bridge over the lower part of the bay. Presently they were on the inland highway again and it was hot, even after the sun went down. They drove until bedtime.

Then, profiting by experience, they did not drive to a hotel but to a garage, parked their car and walked to the hotel, carrying baskets with ferns sticking out and a suitcase with toothbrushes and pajamas. They went to the desk and Rodney wrote "Timotheus T. Pettigrew, Oshkosh, Wis.," and "Pamela Pettigrew, ditto, ditto." They told the clerk that they were botanists and had ferns in their baskets. Since the ferns were in plain sight, they were shown to their rooms without question. They locked the doors and shut the transoms, and turned on the air conditioners and went peacefully to sleep, with no reporters or photographers to haunt their dreams.

Next morning there were the papers, with the story of the press conference and the very dignified and impressive speech which Rodney had made. There was also a picture of him and the royal Abyssinian geese. Some bright theater man had offered the use of his theater as an auction room and it was announced that at three o'clock next Friday afternoon the royal Abyssinian geese would be auctioned off to the highest bidder and the proceeds turned over to the Green Cross.

"And now for Yosemite!" said Rodney. They had another drive up into the mountains. The beautifully graded highway curved this way and that through passes over which nature had scattered trees with lavish hands. They saw some famous scenery—vast gorges and waterfalls, vistas of mountain and lake and stream. They saw forests of many kinds and sizes and drove here and there and searched all day. They spent the night in mountain camps and drove to new places and searched some more. They saw bear and deer and many tourists, but they saw no gnomes, or trace of them. The heart

111

of Glogo sank lower and lower, and strive as he might, he was depressing company.

A curious situation had arisen. Glogo was mourning for the future of his grandson, and the grandson, good and dutiful, tried his best to mourn about himself, but wasn't able to. Bobo, once a loyal and patriotic gnome, had fallen bit by bit under the spell of the big people. He tried to keep it from his grandfather, but the fact was that Bobo liked to eat ripe olives and celery and ice-cream cones. He liked to look out the window and see the cars go by, even at risk of being discovered. He liked to be told what was in the papers.

On Saturday morning, when he heard the account of the auction sale and learned that the only pair of royal Abyssinian geese in America had fetched a price of $2,240, he was far more interested in talking about that money and what could be bought with it than he was in searching for gnomes. Rodney began to wonder—even if they did find the little people, would Bobo want to live with them?

They sat on the edge of a mountain meadow eating their supper, and Glogo said, "There's no use looking any farther. There are no gnomes in Yosemite."

"There are plenty of other national parks," countered Rodney.

So they had another of those arguments in which each tried to be more polite than the other. Glogo said they must go back to the redwoods and not impose on their friends any more. Rodney said it was the most enjoyable adventure of his life. Besides, what would become of the royal Abyssinian goose eggs? They teased the thousand-year-old one until they got him to laughing.

The result was a decision to leave Yosemite and to go eastward, visiting Zion and Bryce Canyon parks. They went back to the "lodge," as the hotel was called, and Rodney put "long distance" to work. Elizabeth talked with Mama and told her what a marvelous time she was having and how she had never once got her feet wet, nor seen anything but very small thunderstorms and no earthquakes at all.

Next morning they rolled out of the mountains and left California, the "hot furnace," behind them. But there were plenty more furnaces in Nevada. The mountains were bare, desolate rocks, scarred and torn into strange shapes and tinted pink and gray and brown and white and many mixtures of these. There would be long stretches of barren land, with nothing but sagebrush and mesquite, already turned brown and gray. The gnomes had never seen such a country or heard of it, and Glogo covered his eyes from it, unable to endure the sufferings of these thirsty plants. He did not have to get out and talk to them—he could tell about them from their tragic aspect.

But the wonderful big people had plenty of water along the highway as well as oil and gas required by the tireless spirit of the gnomobile. Also they had everything for their own needs—sandwiches, hot dogs, soda pop, ice-cream cones. Glogo might be ever so sorrowful, but he had to yield to the spell of the last-named concoction in the midst of the baking heat of Nevada. The ice-cream cone is one of America's contributions to civilization. It comes in three main colors, white, brown, and pink. From Portland, Oregon, to Portland, Maine, it is always the same shape, size, flavor and price. If it were not for its perishable nature it might easily serve the purposes of a medium of exchange.

The highway was no longer paved but "graveled." This

meant that they whirled along in clouds of dust. But it was all behind them—the well-trained gnomobile threw it into the face of the other fellow. However, there wasn't much traffic in this country, and the sagebrush and mesquite got most of the dust. There were bumps in the road and Glogo and Bobo had to use the ropes which had been provided. Bobo found it grand sport to be tossed around and Rodney called him the young gnome on the flying trapeze.

Bobo and Elizabeth had devised games to beguile the tedium of these long drives. They would make bets about the numbers on the license plates of the next car. They hadn't anything to bet but they bet all the same and kept track of their winnings.

They got maps at the filling stations and Bobo was tireless in his study of these. He didn't know how to read, but he was getting Elizabeth to teach him. He could follow the lines indicating the roads and Elizabeth had to tell him the names of all the towns and the distances between. He was learning to recognize the different kinds of gas stations and the different makes of cars—in short, Bobo was becoming a young American, up to the minute in manners, ideas and language, and if they *had* happened to find any gnomes, he would secretly have despised them as a lot of "hicks."

They thought they had heard the last of the royal Abyssinian geese—but not so! In the mining town of Tonopah, Rodney bought a newspaper and read that the geese had been bought by a "vaudeville man," who was hastening to make money by showing them to the public. He had dressed up a girl as an "Abyssinian gooseherd"; she had led the geese onto the stage with varicolored ribbons and danced and sang a

114

comic song about her country. He had set off firecrackers and every time one went off the geese would give a jump and wag their tails. It was reported to have made a great hit with the audience.

Elizabeth asked how the man had been able to train the geese in such a short time and Rodney said perhaps he had an invisible wire running behind the curtains and gave the poor creatures an electric shock. Anyhow it was nice to know that the crowds now had something else to stare at than the gnomobile and its passengers.

Chapter Nine

IN WHICH THE GNOMOBILE GOES EAST

They came into Utah, another state full of mountains, in which the forces of nature had tried many sorts of odd experiments—turning mountains upside down or standing them on their sides; chopping them into building blocks and piling them in strange ways; splitting them down the middle, or digging archways through them.

You could see what you thought must surely be the Chinese wall; then what must be old Indian forts; then the Egyptian sphinx; then a whole block of New York skyscrapers beginning to fall into ruins. You would see a herd of elephants all jammed together, then a fleet of automobiles dissolving into the sky line, then the hanging gardens of Nebuchadnezzar. There would be a place where a giant had come along with a sharp sword, and sliced off the tops of all the mountains, leaving them smooth and level. You imagined it must be nice and green up there, a place for a picnic, only it was a long way off.

Then another giant had come with a box of paints just like Elizabeth's ten-cent box, only bigger. He had dipped his brush into bright pink and painted the cheeks of the cliffs like those of the royal Abyssinian geese. He had painted the tops a bright yellow like an Abyssinian goose's crown.

Or maybe the giants had fought a battle. Here were mountain surfaces of a vivid red, exactly as it would gush from the veins of a giant. The trees had tried to hide the wounds, so there were splotches of red and green. Behind them would be a higher range of mountains, with white splotches—it might be snow and it might be marble, you could not tell. A little farther on nature had tried a new combination and put the white and green hills in the foreground and the red and green mountains behind them. Or maybe it would be black ones, brown ones, gray ones, or shades and blendings of these.

The road wound this way and that, through such strange sights. The gnomobile would climb and come over a summit and you would have hundreds of miles of mountain chains spread out before your eyes. You would go down and the great cliffs would come rushing out in front of the gnomobile and try to block its path. Then it would have to dodge or maybe slice off the edge of a hill or maybe dive straight through. Glogo and Bobo would be worried, not being used to rushing head on into mountains at fifty miles an hour. But always the road had got there ahead of them and fixed everything up. Day or night made no difference to this magic.

They came to Bryce Canyon, packed with strange sights like this, and then to Zion Park. They dutifully got out and plunged into forests and searched for gnomes—but in vain. So once more Glogo sank down and plunged his head into his hands and Rodney had to apply his neurasthenia cure. "Oh, but you haven't seen Colorado yet!"

He started to sing the wonders of Colorado mountains and Colorado forests—you would have thought the Colorado Chamber of Commerce was talking or the Denver and Rio Grande Railroad. As a matter of fact it was, for Rodney had stopped in a railroad depot and got a folder. From it he had acquired the information that the word "colorado" means red and that one of the steps of the state capitol is exactly one mile above sea level. Bobo, the perfect tourist, was thrilled. Glogo, seeing this, controlled his grief and said, "All right, go on."

They drove east, and presently it was Colorado. In the Rocky Mountain National Park they made another search. In the tilted strata which make up these mountains Rodney said there were rocks full of petrified bark and leaves of giant sequoias which had flourished forty million years ago. There might be the bones of gnomes also. But that didn't cheer up Glogo—he wasn't looking for any petrified gnomes but for one live young lady gnome to marry his grandson.

And now what were they going to do about it? They had come all the way through the mountains of the West and had had no luck. If they turned back, it would mean a complete surrender to the dark powers of neurasthenia. Glogo would crawl into his basket and lie there and not even an ice-cream cone could tempt him out.

Rodney and Elizabeth had talked it over and come to a decision. In one of their grand councils with the gnomes, they began to tell about the wonders to be found in Minnesota and Wisconsin—no mountains there, but beautiful lakes and in the northern part virgin forests in which great companies of gnomes might dwell. To be sure, said Rodney, they would have to cross the plains. It was a long trip, apt to be hot, and they would see no trees except cottonwoods in the river bottoms. But they would drive fast and do it in a couple of days. Glogo could stay in his basket and confer with the spirit of the gnomobile.

Said Glogo, "I have been listening to the spirit, and it tells me that it is not altogether happy. It may be the beginning of neurasthenia."

"Good gracious, I didn't know it was contagious!" exclaimed Rodney. In town he had a garage mechanic examine the car and found that the man who had done the last greasing job had failed to tighten one of the bolts of the transmission and the grease had nearly all leaked out. Rodney said that Glogo's "incog" name should be changed from General Grant to Lord High Chief Trouble Shooter. He said that a gnome in the back seat would very soon be standard equipment for all motorcars.

They were setting out on a new journey. "Minnesota or bust" was their motto, said Rodney. "Eastward the star of gnompire takes its way." He was full of nonsense like that. He would ask old Grandpa Glogo many questions, some of them serious and some of them funny, keeping him talking all the time. In the hotel at night Rodney made notes of the different things Glogo told him.

He was going to write a book, he said. It would be called *Gnome News* and of course would have to be published in Alaska. When Elizabeth asked why, Rodney said he was ashamed to explain, because a pun is the lowest form of wit. There was a city in Alaska called Nome, he had to explain to Bobo.

Rodney called Mama on long distance and told where they

were and where they wanted to go. Of course, Mama was horrified—what had been the sense of bringing Elizabeth out west if Rodney was going to take her right back east again? Rodney said that was easy—how could she have started back east until she had got west? It was more of his nonsense.

Elizabeth pleaded—she was having the *most* lovely time and it was the only time in all her long life that she had had any fun out of getting educated. Mama was suspicious of any education that wasn't a bore—she had never got any such in her time. But it so happened that Mama was having a good time herself, so she said all right and told Elizabeth not to say "O.K." because it was horrid—the way the gangsters talked in the movies. Elizabeth said she hadn't been to a single movie, she was so much more interested in talking to Professor Glogo. So Mama knew that her little daughter's culture was really being improved.

They set out next morning, very happy and all excited about Minnesota. Rodney chose this occasion to reveal that he had written a poem about Bobo and his problem. Rodney frequently wrote poems, but he seldom got them published. They were too easy to understand, he said, and nothing was considered to be a poem nowadays if anybody could understand it. Elizabeth couldn't understand that and Rodney explained that the poets wanted to be different from a world which they didn't like and they had come to be so different that they couldn't understand themselves.

Anyhow, here was the poem about Bobo.

> I know a forest dim and stilled
> Where towering trees a temple build;
> And in that forest lives a gnome,

He sorrows in his ancient home;
The axes lay the forest low,
And where's a little gnome to go?
He's young—a thousand years of life
Confront him, and he wants a wife.
But all the gnomes have gone away,
And who's to tell him where they stay?
Only one kind of man may know it;
He brings his burden to a poet.
Lovers of woodlands one and all,
Wherever you may hear my call:
Go spread the word, seek high, seek low,
Wherever ferns and mosses grow;
And if you find a lady gnome
I offer her a happy home.

Elizabeth clapped her hands with delight. She said there just couldn't be a nicer poem than that. Rodney said it was practical too. He explained to Glogo that it wouldn't be giving away their secret, for the average person would take the poem as just a piece of foolishness, while the true forest lovers would understand and make a search. It might be there was someone who already had a collection of gnomes and was hiding them for the same reasons that Rodney and Elizabeth were doing it.

Glogo said it was all right to go ahead and publish the poem but he didn't expect anything from it, because he couldn't believe there were many forest lovers among the big people—else why were they willing to let the trees be cut down and turned into ugly wooden boxes? If they had to have boxes to live in, why at least couldn't they always plant another tree?

So then Rodney and Glogo had a long talk about what was called "conservation." Rodney said that people had learned by now to take care of their forests and only allowed trees to be cut when they had got to a certain size and always required that new ones be planted. He said the lumber business didn't have to be just blind greed, that would destroy itself along with everything else in the world.

Glogo thought it was too late—the soil had been washed off so many mountains and hills and you couldn't put it back any more than you could put the gnomes back. The old grandfather crawled into his basket and had an especially bad fit of despair.

They came out of the mountains and through the foot-hills and onto rolling plains where cattle grazed. You came down little by little, hardly knowing that you were descending, so it did not make your ears crackle and choke up. They were following what was at first a stream, and presently became a sandy river. It was called the Platte and Rodney said it was famous because it had been the home of William Jennings Bryan, known as "the boy-orator" in the old days. His enemies had said that his speeches were like his river, six hundred miles long, a mile wide, and one foot deep. Rodney had been reading a book about those old days and explained the political battle which had shaken the nation. It had been about money, a subject which seemed to Glogo the craziest of all the affairs of the big people.

Glogo was interested in the river and its color. "Oh, look!" he exclaimed. "It's yellow! It's yellow!" He kept saying that. It seemed to him a dreadful thing that a river should be allowed to have a color and that nobody paid any attention to it. It meant that the world was coming to an end. All that dirt or silt or whatever men chose to call it was the stuff out of which life was made, and it was being swept down into the ocean, where never again would it be of any use.

They sped on and it was hot. The lower they went, the hotter it got. This was another result of murdering the forests, said Glogo. Rodney said he didn't think there ever had been forests on these plains, but the old gnome said there might be, if the big people would use their knowledge to take care of the earth.

The fields had been plowed and corn planted, and it was young and bright green and pretty to look at. Rodney explained what corn was and how it grew and how it tasted. Glogo said that no one should treat the land that way unless it was flat. If it had a slope, the soil was washed away and no one should be allowed to plant anything on a slope except trees or something that would bind the soil.

Rodney expressed surprise that Glogo had worked out the principles of "conservation" all by himself, but the old gnome said all his people had known it. The gnomes had ventured to the edge of the forest and watched what the big people were doing. They had seen plowing and planting and what it did to the soil. They had seen clear mountain streams turned into muddy rivers. Who but a man crazed with greed could fail to care?

"U.S. 30" said the highway signs. Rodney said it was called the Lincoln Highway and he told about Lincoln and what he had done to free the slaves. It was as good as going to school to listen to one who had read so many books. Neither Glogo nor Bobo had ever heard of people with dark skins, and when they passed one on the road they gazed with great interest. The dark man gazed back at the tiny faces and must have thought he was bewitched.

They passed many curious and interesting sights, which had to be explained to the gnomes. There were caravans of new automobiles, all with numbers painted on them, being driven to the California market. Some of them were loaded onto big trucks, six to a truck. There were old cars, loaded with family belongings and babies and chickens, following the star of empire. They saw young men having joy rides, a lady getting a sun bath, her bare feet hanging out of the window of the car, an old farmer on his way to town sitting up straight in the driver's seat, and his wife in the back seat cutting his hair. Such queer sights gave them topics for gay conversation.

When they came out of a town, there would be young men holding up their thumbs at them. Rodney, as part of the neurasthenia cure, invented the tale that this was a signal of friendship and good wishes. Bobo thought it was a pleasant custom, and would have returned the greeting if he had not been told to keep out of sight.

It was Nebraska now and more and more fields were plowed. This was the "corn belt," Rodney explained. It grew hotter and hotter. There were fields of winter wheat, now ripening fast. The landscape had become a series of farms, each with a small house and a big barn and silo and a few trees around it. The country rolled endlessly and as you came over one little ridge you saw several new ridges before you.

125

They stopped in a town to buy food for supper and then they stopped under some trees by the roadside to eat. When they got through, Elizabeth chanced to look behind them and saw a vast black cloud that seemed to cover the whole horizon. It wasn't a thundercloud, for it came right down to the ground, and it was even and uniform, not billowing and rolling. They stopped at the next filling station to ask and the man said, "One o' them dusters; she's comin' fast."

Rodney said he wasn't going to be caught in any "duster." The gnomobile could travel faster than the wind, unless it was a hurricane. He got more gas and water and told the spirit to get a move on, and away they went at a mile a minute across the State of Nebraska. The black cloud stayed on the horizon behind them; it didn't get nearer and there was no dust in the air.

By and by it was dark. You could no longer see the corn-fields or the new wheatfields or the farmhouses with their trees. Everything was mysterious, except on the highway ahead, where the gnomobile shot its shaft of light. The wind-shield was tilted and a fresh breeze blew through—a special private breeze made by and for themselves.

The gnomes were tired and crept into their baskets. By and by Elizabeth became tired and climbed into the back seat and put a pillow under her head and went to sleep. But Rodney sat in the driver's seat, staring out ahead, thinking his own thoughts. He was used to driving and did not tire and he won the race with the duster. When Elizabeth opened her eyes again they were in a garage and about to go to a motel.

Chapter Ten

IN WHICH THE GOSLINGS STEP OUT

Next day they were in Iowa. They were bright and eager again—Glogo at least pretending to be for the sake of good manners. This was the "breadbasket of America," said Rodney—also the ham-sandwich basket. Most of the farms had fields with big black and brown hogs in them. Rodney said that every farmer in the state of Iowa was required by law to raise fifty thousand hogs and then he was permitted to move to California. Bobo wanted to know what became of the hogs and Rodney said that other people ate them. Bobo asked what the farmers got for it and Rodney said, a mortgage. It was more of his foolishness. It had to do with money, which Glogo said was the foolishness of all the big people put together.

They turned north and little by little the country began to change. There were more hills having woods upon their slopes. The farms were smaller, with fruit orchards and fields with cows in them. They were passing out of the corn belt and into the dairy country. Presently there were little lakes and these had woods all around them. It was cooler and that made life easier for the gnomes.

Bobo was hopping from one side of the car to the other to see the new sights. Bobo never tired of watching the highway dodging this way and that through the hills. Every day the world grew bigger; every day the big people grew more wonderful. Poor old Glogo felt out of it entirely. He would crawl back into his basket and nurse his grief in silence while Bobo and Elizabeth chattered about a new game they had invented—counting the cows. Bobo had one side of the road and Elizabeth the other and when they came to big herds the gnomobile had to slow up in order that one or the other might not lose his full score.

So far on their journey they had had bright sunshine, almost too much of it. But now heavy clouds rolled up and it began to rain. The gnomobile moved more slowly over the

wet pavement and the water streamed down the window glass. Bobo never lost his pleasure in watching it. A wonderful thing—to be so near to the rain and yet be safe and dry. That had been one of the difficulties in the life of a gnome, it appeared. When you got wet, you had to stay wet. Even old Glogo had to admit that it was pleasanter to stay dry.

Then there was the magical little thing called the "windshield wiper," which worked incessantly in front of Rodney's face! Was it the spirit of the gnomobile or was it a separate spirit, all to itself? And how did it know when rains began? Did it feel the wet or had Rodney told it? The water poured down in blinding torrents but the valiant windshield wiper never lost heart. It pumped away faster and faster, throwing the water to this side and that.

They came to a little river and it had risen to a flood that went rushing under a bridge. It was a dark brown and looked like boiling mud. "There!" cried Glogo. "See what you do when you murder the trees!" He would point out little streams here and there, flowing down the hillsides, bearing the soil with them. It hurt him, as if he were a miser and all this was precious gold that belonged to him. It was going on everywhere, all over the country, every time it rained—and nobody cared!

The rain continued to pour down and presently there was water over the road and Rodney had to drive still more slowly and carefully. Then there were flat fields ahead and the yellow water lay over them like a lake. They saw a lot of cars ahead and men moving about in the rain and when they got to the place and inquired, they learned that a bridge had been washed out ahead. The water was rising and people were

having to be taken out of farmhouses in boats. Rodney had
to turn the gnomobile about and creep back over the road he
had come.

All the time the thousand-year-old one was working himself into a frenzy, almost crying with pain because of what
the big people had done—chopping down all the trees and
letting the land be destroyed! They had dust storms and the
precious topsoil was blown away by the wind. They had
floods and it was borne off by the water. All summer long
they had heat waves, and could only keep themselves alive
with electric fans and air conditioners and ice-cream cones
and racing about the country at a mile a minute to make a
breeze!

They retraced several miles and took a new road. They
got across the raging river by a bridge which was still standing but in grave danger because there was a piece of a big red
barn pounding against it and another piece drifting down
on it. Rodney was much ashamed to have the old gnome see
such sights and had to admit that the big people were handling
their affairs very badly indeed. He was glad when they got
out of this valley and up into the northern part of the state,
which the greed of the lumbermen had not yet entirely
ruined. Here were real forests and after the rain the most
heavenly coolness. Every tiny point of every green fern was
dripping with shining jewels, and there was a soft mist rising
out of the velvet forest floor.

This was a country where it was again possible to think of
gnomes, so they got out and went hunting some more. There
were no giant trees as in California, but there were good big
fellows and many of them. There were forest twilight and

the magic smell of balsam and the singing of wind overhead
and green ferns and flowers—all the things which gnomes
love. Glogo and Bobo hunted like bloodhounds on a scent,
but they found no traces of their little people.

They went on to the very top of the state, into the Pigeon
River country, where they found real virgin forests. They
spent many days there, moving from place to place over

wilderness roads. Nowhere did they find any trace of gnomes
and the poor old thousand-year one sank into ever deeper
grief. To save him, Rodney had to take all the blame upon
himself. "I fear I have made a mistake," he said. "I over-
looked the fact that the winters up here are severe and maybe
the gnomes couldn't stand them."

Glogo had to forgive him and give him another chance.
They would find some forests in a warmer part of the country. Rodney had in mind the Ozark Mountains about which
he had read in some magazine. They would go there and
have a look. It would be hot on the way to Arkansas, but
they would have ice-cold thermos bottles and get only air-
conditioned hotel rooms and all day the obliging spirit of the
gnomobile would make a mile-a-minute gale for them. So
Rodney talked, trying desperately to keep from having to
admit that his neurasthenia cure was a failure!

Glogo had got to the point where he didn't argue—all
right, whatever his big friends pleased. Bobo had got to the
point where any part of America was delightful, provided it
was a new part and he could ask questions about it. So they
started south again, and before long had come to the Mis-
sissippi River, a name which the gnomes somehow found very
hard to say. It got more and more depressing to Glogo the
bigger it got because it was bearing larger and larger quanti-
ties of mud to places where it would never again be of any
use to gnomes or men.

There were cities along this river, and one morning in a
town of Missouri befell an accident which knocked all their
plans upside down. Rodney had been carrying out his promise
to Mama to drive carefully. But there was no way he could

134

keep a man in a hurry from starting across ahead of a traffic signal and hitting the gnomobile a sideswipe and smashing its fender and knocking one of its rear wheels crooked.

The gnomes were in their baskets and got jostled and scared, but not hurt. Nor was the gnomobile seriously hurt. It could be taken to a hospital and fixed up in a few hours, Rodney said. The real seriousness developed a minute later, when a policeman came pushing through the crowd and insisted upon arresting the man who had run into Rodney. As part of his official duty the policeman had to note down the license number of Rodney's car, and his name and address. While he was writing, a sudden idea struck him and he began to stare at the young man. "Sinsabow? Sinsabow? Haven't I heard that name somewhere?"

"It's not a very common name," said Rodney, with the guilty feeling of a check forger or bank robber.

"But I think I read something about Rodney Sinsabow in the paper. Oh, I know! The royal Abyssinian geese! Ain't you the gentleman that owned them geese?"

Rodney had to admit that he was the one—for how could he know the laws of Missouri and the penalty for telling a fib to a policeman?

"Well! Well!" said the cop. "I'm glad to meet you, sir. That was an interesting story. It's too bad about them poor geese."

"You mean their going on the stage?"

"No, I mean the way they died."

"Oh! Did they die?"

"Didn't you read about it in the paper?"

"No, I missed it."

"Well, there was a fire in the theater and they got burned up."

"Oh, dear!" exclaimed Rodney. "That's terrible! And after all the time I spent teaching them!"

"But didn't you have some o' the eggs, Mr. Sinsabow?"

"Yes, I had some."

"That's what the paper said. They was trying to find where you was and what become o' them eggs."

"Indeed!" said Rodney, feeling like the check forger or the bank robber when the handcuffs are closing upon his wrists.

"Whatever become o' them eggs, Mr. Sinsabow?"

"They're in a safe place."

"Must be time for 'em to hatch, ain't it?"

"Just about, yes."

"Then you'll have some royal Abyssinian goslin's, won't you?"

"I hope so."

"Well, them birds ought to be worth a lot o' money. Take care o' them."

A crowd had gathered, listening to the conversation, and getting the thrill of something far more important than a collision of two cars. The average American reads about world events but he may pass all his days without ever coming face to face with a real "celebrity." When he does, he is seized by an overpowering impulse. Every man in that crowd realized that if he shook hands with Rodney he would have something to tell to everyone he met for weeks afterward. "Yes, I met him and he says to me, says he—"

So there was the poor lumber scion, shy and exclusive in his tastes, caught with a crippled gnomobile, which had to be pushed out of the way of traffic. He had to stand and keep guard over it until a tow car came and took it to a gnomobile hospital, after which he and his niece had to take their baskets to a hotel and get a room and wait until the car surgeon had performed his operation.

Of course, Rodney wrote their "incog" names, "Timotheus T. Pettigrew" and "Pamela Pettigrew." This time he did it without much hope. He knew that the policeman would talk at the station house—and newspaper reporters always keep in touch with police stations. It would be easy for a reporter, once put on the trail, to find out where the gnomobile had been taken; and when he learned that the travelers had carried two large wicker baskets, it would be easy to find the hotel at which they had sought refuge. Rodney knew by now that hotels are always on the side of reporters.

So he was not surprised when the phone rang, and a polite voice inquired, "Is this Mr. Sinsabow?"

"You must have the wrong room," said Rodney.

"Is this Mr. Pettigrew, then?"

"Yes, this is Mr. Pettigrew."

"Well, Mr. Pettibow—pardon me, Mr. Sinsagrew—I am a reporter for the *Evening Sizzle-Hoot,* our local newspaper and I would like to ask you about the royal Abyssinian goslings."

"I am sorry," said Rodney, "but I am too hot."

"Too hot, Mr. Pettibow?"

"Yes, I am sizzling hot. Also I am hooting."

"Oh, I see—ha! ha! ha! But really, Mr. Sinsapet, you can't imagine the excitement of the world over the royal Abyssinian goslings. Every newspaper in the country has been trying to find you. Will you tell me whether all the eggs hatched and have you got thirteen goslings?"

"The goslings are sizzling hot, too and they are all hooting."

"Have you got them in those baskets, Mr. Pettisin?"

"I have ferns in the baskets."

"But please, Mr. Abbysin, tell me, have you got the thirteen goslings on top of the ferns?"

"I'm sorry I haven't time to talk with you. Make up the story for yourself."

"Oh, but really, Mr. Abbygrew—"

"Yes, you can do it much better than I. You are in practice."

"Do you really mean that?"

"What difference does it make whether I mean it or not?" Rodney hung up the receiver and Elizabeth and Bobo sizzled with laughter and also they hooted. When they tried to guess what the reporter would make up, they sizzled and hooted some more. Bobo thought the newspapers of the big people had delightful names—first the *Whizzle-Bang* and then the *Fizzle-Toot* and then the *Sizzle-Hoot!*

It was then about noon and Rodney said the story would be on the street in a couple of hours. After that they would have to get out of town. He went over to the gnomobile hospital to see how the surgical operation was coming along. When he came back it was with a grave face. The injuries had proved to be more serious than expected and it was necessary to send to a nearby city for a new rear axle. It would be impossible to have the gnomobile in shape before evening. "We'll have another siege with the photographers," said the lumber scion. "I've picked out a fat man down in the lobby."

Rodney had brought some food—for, of course, they couldn't take the gnomes into a restaurant. They ate their lunch. Before they were through the bell rang again and it was the correspondent of a press association wanting to know the names of the thirteen royal Abyssinian goslings. Rodney said, "All right, have you got a pencil ready?" He started to dictate, "Alpha, Beta, Gamma, Delta, Epsilon, Zeta, Eta, Theta—I forget the next one, but if you have a Greek grammar in the office, you can look it up—Kappa, Lambda, Mu, Nu, Omicron—" These are letters of the Greek alphabet and from the first two we get our word "alphabet."

"But that makes fourteen, Mr. Sinsabow."

"Well, then, there isn't any Omicron."

The reporter wanted to know if the goslings had cut their eyeteeth yet. Rodney said he had already put a reporter to work on those details and if he let two work on them, they might not agree. Unfortunately, Rodney hadn't got the first man's name, but the story would be out very soon, and whatever it was, it was right. Then Rodney hung up, and told the hotel office not to call him any more and he hung out the "Do Not Disturb" sign on the doorknob.

After an hour or two Rodney went down and got an afternoon paper. There was another of those fantastic yarns which had set the whole country to chuckling. The reporter told how the eccentric young lumber millionaire had built himself an incubator in the back part of his expensive automobile and had hatched the royal Abyssinian goose eggs while making a tour of the United States. He now had thirteen royal Abyssinian goslings in two large wicker baskets, bedded on ferns which he had brought from the high Sierras.

All these tiny creatures had pink cheeks and golden crowns, like their late lamented parents. They had already been trained to wag their tails and answer questions and were on their way to a famous surgeon to have their tongues cleft in order that they might be taught to talk. The lumber scion valued them at two thousand dollars a pair and said he was going to donate them to the Green Cross when his course of training was completed.

After Elizabeth and Bobo had done their laughing over that story, they had to get down to the serious problem of how to get away from the reporters. Because of their license plates from the State of Washington, they would be known in every town and would be followed and have no peace in any hotel. Elizabeth said the would have to go out into the country and buy thirteen goslings and paint them up and have another auction sale. Glogo said that he could not endure to be the cause of so much trouble and expense to his friends—what they should do was to go back at once to the redwoods. But Rodney said, nonsense, he had never had so much fun in his life—it was a game he was playing with the newspapers. Bobo and Elizabeth were loud in their agreement, so the thousand-year-old one retired to his basket.

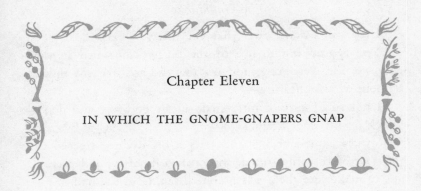

Chapter Eleven

IN WHICH THE GNOME-GNAPERS GNAP

They were still in the midst of discussing plans to get to the
Ozark Mountains, when there came a tap upon the door.
Bobo popped into his basket and Elizabeth pulled the covers
over both of them. Rodney went to the door but did not
open it. "Who is there?" he demanded.

"Somebody to see Mr. Pettigrew," said a man's voice.

"Don't you see I have a sign out, 'Do Not Disturb'?"

"But this is very urgent, Mr. Pettigrew."

"What do you want?"

"Won't you please let me talk to you, just a moment?"

"What do you want to talk about?"

"I want to buy the royal Abyssinian goslings."

"They are not for sale."

"I'll pay you your full price, Mr. Pettigrew—thirteen
thousand dollars for the lot."

"I'm not interested."

"Certified check, Mr. Pettigrew—or cash if you prefer."

"I have no goslings for sale."

"I might raise the offer, Mr. Pettigrew."

"I tell you I don't care what you offer."

"You are talking to one of the biggest showmen in the country, Mr. Pettigrew, and it's too bad to turn me down without at least hearing—"

"I tell you I am not interested. Please go away and don't knock on my door again."

So there came a silence and after a bit Rodney tiptoed to the door of the other room, and opened it softly, and peeped out to make sure there was no one listening in the hall.

They resumed their discussion of how to escape the reporters and other exasperaters. Rodney said he would go and arrange to get some more money—without which it was impossible to escape any troubles in the world of the big people. He cautioned Elizabeth to stay with the gnomes and in no case to open the door of either room. Then he hurried off.

Elizabeth and Bobo never failed to have a good time whenever they were together. Bobo asked so many questions about the big world and required so many explanations that it was an education for a little girl to try to satisfy him. Now he wanted to know all about showmen, what they were and what they showed and where and how. Did they make money, and how much? Elizabeth had a hard time answering questions like that!

Rodney came back, having got his money. He had brought some supper. They ate, and then played jacks for a while, after which Rodney went over to see how the repairs to the gnomobile were coming on. Again he cautioned his niece to stay with the gnomes and not to open the door.

A few minutes passed and Elizabeth and Bobo were in the midst of a game, when the telephone rang and she answered.

Suddenly she gave a cry of terror and turned white. There was a man's voice on the phone and it said, "Your Uncle Rodney has been run over by an automobile. You must come quickly."

"Oh, where, where?" cried Elizabeth. The voice answered, "On Main Street, a couple of blocks west of the hotel. Come right away."

Elizabeth dropped the receiver. She almost fainted with fright and grief. "Oh, Bobo! Glogo! Rodney has been run over by a car! Maybe he's dead!"

"Can we go too?" cried Bobo. She said, "No, no, you can't go out onto the street. Wait here, and I'll come back as soon as I can." And without waiting to put on her hat she dashed out of the room, shutting the door behind her.

She couldn't even bear to wait for the elevator, but ran down a couple of flights of stairs, and through the lobby, and out onto the street. "Which is Main Street?" she asked of the first passerby, and then, "Which is west?" Down the street she rushed, sobbing, choking, beside herself with fright.

She ran two blocks, then stopped and looked about. She expected to see a crowd, but there was no crowd and no sign of anything unusual on any of the four corners. She looked in every direction, and finally rushed to a man who had a newsstand at the corner. "My uncle!" she cried. "Where is he?" Then, seeing the man looked puzzled: "He was run over by an automobile."

"Where?" asked the man.

"At this corner—so I was told."

"There hasn't anybody been run over here," said the man. "Not since I been here."

"I was told it was on Main Street, two blocks west of the Traveler's Hotel."

"Well, that's here," said the man, "but they musta got it wrong, nobody's been run over here. Who told you?"

"Someone telephoned. Oh, it must be near here!" And Elizabeth, looking up and down the street, suddenly gave a loud cry: "Rodney! Rodney!" and started to run as fast as she could. There was her uncle, coming up the street, walking, and seeming entirely well.

He turned when he heard her cry. "Oh, Rodney, Rodney! Were you hurt?"

"Hurt?" said he, looking puzzled.

"I was told you had been run over."

"Me? Who told you?" Rodney's voice was full of sudden alarm.

"Someone telephoned to the hotel."

"Who?"

"I don't know—a man."

"And you left the gnomes alone?"

"What could I do, Rodney? They said for me to come to you."

"Come!" cried Rodney. He started off, not waiting for Elizabeth, but running as fast as he could. Elizabeth followed but he was far ahead of her. He was upstairs in the room when she got there.

One glance at his face was enough to make her heart almost stop beating. "They're gone!" said Rodney.

"Oh! Oh!" cried Elizabeth and she started to scream, "Bobo! Glogo!"

"No use," said Rodney. "I've looked everywhere. They're gone."

"But, Rodney! Where?"

"They've been stolen. Don't you see—it was a trick to get you out of the way."

Elizabeth put her hands to her face and burst into weeping. Rodney went and closed the door and the child threw herself on the bed, sobbing as if her heart would break. "Oh, Bobo! Glogo!" She cried their names again and again. She could not believe that her little friends were not somewhere in the rooms. But Rodney told her he had searched everywhere. The baskets were there, but the gnomes had been taken.

The child sat up, with her streaming eyes. "Rodney, we must find them! We must tell the police!"

"We can't, dear."

"Why not?"

"Don't you see for yourself? Can we tell the police that we had two gnomes in our car?"

"Why not?"

"They'll think it's a silly hoax. Nobody believes in gnomes."

"Then you mean—they're gone forever?"

"I don't mean that. I think we can find them, but not through the police. You may be sure that whoever stole them has a car and is on the way to some other city."

"But, Rodney, they'll die! How wicked! How dreadful!"

"No, dear, I don't think we have to worry about that. They'll be taken good care of."

"How can you know that?"

"They're too valuable."

"For what?"

"For show purposes. The goslings were worth a thousand dollars but the gnomes will be worth a million. Anyone who has them will see that no harm comes to them."

"But, Rodney, how will they live without us?"

Elizabeth started another fit of weeping. Rodney told her that wouldn't do any good. They must keep their heads and think what to do for their little friends.

"It's easy to see what happened," said he. "That showman tried to buy the goslings and when he couldn't, he set out to steal them or hired someone else to do it. No doubt the thief brought a box or a suitcase or something and he had a passkey to get into the room. Of course when he saw the gnomes, he knew that he had something far more precious."

"Oh, Rodney. The poor little things will be terrified."

"I don't think so," said Rodney. "Glogo doesn't care much what happens to him and as for Bobo, he knows his way about by now. The man will soon make them understand that he doesn't mean them any harm."

Elizabeth started another fit of weeping, blaming herself because of the stupid thing she had done. But Rodney said the trick had been a clever one and she could hardly have acted otherwise. Indeed, when Elizabeth remembered the terror and despair she had felt when she thought that Rodney might be dead, she was almost happy again!

It seemed a wrong to their little friends that they should sit there and do nothing in such a situation. But Rodney said that if they spread an alarm, they might drive the criminals to desperation. It would be easy for them to make away with the two little people and bury the bodies or they might hide them and carry them to some foreign country. But if Rodney and Elizabeth waited, the thieves might get the idea that they were not so much interested in the little people and not disposed to make a scandal.

Rodney talked with his niece, asking her opinion just as if she were a grown-up person. He did this to comfort her and divert her mind, for in truth he felt, just as she did, the gap that was left in their lives by the absence of Glogo and Bobo.

The hotel rooms did not seem the same; the gnomobile would not seem the same. Rodney had to keep talking, and make jokes. He said he had read about kidnapers, but never before about gnome-gnapers!

The way to get track of the gnomes would be to employ a detective agency. Undoubtedly that "showman" was the thief or employer of the thief. It ought to be easy to learn if there had been a showman staying in this town. What was his name and where had he stayed? Had he announced himself at the hotel desk before he came up to knock on Rodney's door? Had he bribed one of the hotel servants? All these problems a detective should know how to solve.

And what would the man do with the gnomes? He could only make money by exhibiting them somewhere and that would soon become known. If he announced them as gnomes, there would be a big sensation and the papers all over the country would be full of it. Even if he called them dwarfs, they were the smallest dwarfs ever known and would attract wide attention. There were trade papers of the show business in which one could find news of what was going on and sooner or later there was bound to be comment on these mysterious little creatures.

Elizabeth began to weep again. What a dreadful thing, to think of their little friends in a circus or a museum—or what would it be? Rodney said he didn't think it would worry Bobo and as for Glogo, one place was as good as another to him. "I wouldn't say it to him, of course, but between you and me, I don't believe there are any more gnomes and I don't think Bobo wants to be a gnome anyhow. Glogo will be less and less pleased with his grandson."

Elizabeth agreed that all this was correct. So Rodney went to the telephone and called the head of a detective agency in St. Louis. He arranged for them to send a couple of "operatives" at once. The men would drive to the town and might be expected in a couple of hours.

"And now," said Rodney, "what we have to do is to get rid of that gosling business. The lobby is full of people waiting for a chance to stare at us and we don't want it."

He phoned to the city editor of the *Sizzle-Hoot,* and told him that he would be pleased to see a reporter. When the man came, Rodney made another of his dignified little speeches. He said that he didn't like confusion and crowds, and neither did the goslings. They were delicate little creatures, easily frightened and not used to publicity. So Rodney had taken them to a farm belonging to a friend of his, and arranged for them to stay there and have a simple country life, with plenty of fresh air and sunshine and all the milk and butter and eggs and fresh fruits and vegetables that goslings need. When they were older, Rodney would teach them and train them and finally turn them over to the Green Cross. That was the story and Rodney hoped the newspapers and the public would respect the rights of the goslings to privacy.

Of course, the reporter wanted to know where this farm was and Rodney said he was very sorry, but to tell that would defeat the purpose. The man wanted to know if it was in this neighborhood. Rodney said the man might do his own guessing. All he wanted was to satisfy the press that the goslings were not in his rooms. Rodney had taken the pillows out of the baskets but left the ferns in and he now showed them to the reporter and invited him to search the rooms and satisfy himself that there were no hidden goslings. Rodney said he hoped the public would forget about him. The reporter went away.

Two heavy-set and serious-looking gentlemen soon made their appearance with cards proving them to be the "operatives" from St. Louis. Smith and Guggins were their names and their eyes opened wide when the lumber scion informed them that the "royal Abyssinian geese" and the "royal Abyssinian goslings" which had been front-page stories all over the country for the past month had been a "blind" to conceal two little dwarfs who had been seeing the country in the lumber scion's car. When the two men were told that there were two creatures in human form, only fourteen or fifteen inches high, and yet adult and able to walk about and speak

the English language, they were not quite certain whether this was a serious assignment or another practical joke of a young man with more money than brains.

Said Rodney, "I am not at liberty to tell you where we found Glogo and Bobo. But they exist and they have been stolen and I want to find them. Apart from what I shall owe your employers, there will be a thousand dollars for each of you if and when you help me to find them." That had a businesslike sound. Rodney went on to tell what clues he had. The men agreed that he had acted wisely in keeping things quiet and said they would set to work at once and report everything they could find out.

It proved to be an easy case. A visit to the city editor of the newspaper brought the information that a well-known "showman," Mr. Morris Quaxton, had been visiting the town. He was the owner of a chain of small motion-picture theaters with headquarters in Chicago and the paper had published a story about him, with his picture, which made it easy. As it happened, he had been staying at the Traveler's Hotel, which made it easier yet.

Back at the hotel one of the operatives introduced himself as an independent picture man, looking for Mr. Quaxton, and learned that the gentleman had "checked out" a couple of hours previously. With him had been registered a Mr. Charles Willowby and he also had departed. The operative got a description of both the gentlemen. Meanwhile the other operative found the garage at which Quaxton had parked his car and learned he had no one with him when he left. Following the guess that a wealthy and important man would not risk his own safety by stealing some goslings, the opera-

The Gnomobile

tive inquired among dealers in secondhand cars and learned
that a man who looked like Willowby had purchased a small
car, giving the name of Alfred Post, and had driven away in
it late that afternoon.

The operatives came back to report to Rodney and Elizabeth. There was not much doubt, they said, that Willowby
had stolen the dwarfs and that Quaxton had got him to do it,
expecting to make money out of showing what he thought
were the royal Abyssinian goslings. The question was, what
did Rodney want done about it?

Rodney answered promptly that he wanted to recover the
gnomes—that is, the dwarfs. Rodney saw by the quick glance
of Smith and Guggins that they had noted his slip but they
said nothing. Did he want to send the men to jail, they asked.
He said, no, he only wanted to rescue his little friends. The
detectives said that made it easier—the other fellows wouldn't
fight so hard.

Smith went to talk with a chambermaid at the hotel. He
told a sad story about poor little Elizabeth who had been
brought up all her life with two little crippled dwarfs and
she loved them so that she was about to die of grief because
they had been stolen. She didn't want anybody punished and
if the chambermaid would help her, they would promise not
to say a word about it and here was a twenty-dollar bill with
the compliments of the little girl. Thus persuaded, the chambermaid confessed that Mr. Willowby had told her that he
was a secret-service operative and that Rodney was not really
a young millionaire, but a dangerous forger in disguise, and
that what he had in the two baskets was the means of making

152

bad money. Persuaded by ten dollars of good money, the chambermaid had given him the key to Rodney's room.

That settled it. Rodney said: "We're off for Chicago." The operatives agreed that that was the next move. To his niece Rodney remarked: "We shall gnap the gnome-gnapers!"

Chapter Twelve

IN WHICH THE GNOME-GNAPERS ARE GNAPED

Next morning the gnomobile was ready, and the expedition set out. They took the two baskets—and, oh, how empty they did seem and how empty the gnomobile, with silence in the back seat all day! Nobody for Elizabeth to count cows with! Nobody to ask questions about all the unusual things they passed on the highway!

However, there was plenty to think about in this new adventure. Elizabeth, of course, had been to the movies and so she knew quite a lot about criminals—what they look like and how they talk and where they live. She knew the various methods of following them and capturing them. And now here she was in a real movie, playing a real detective, and with two more of them following her in another car. Impossible not to be thrilled by such an adventure! Elizabeth put away childish things, such as betting on the numbers of car licenses, and adopted the worldly manner of a girl-sleuth.

Where would "one of the biggest showmen in America" keep a pair of captive gnomes? Who would take care of them for him and where and how? Would he beat them and

frighten them or would he try to please them and win their
confidence? At what kind of place would he plan to exhibit
them and what kind of people would come to him with business offers? You had to know a lot of different things if you
were going to be a successful "dick."

Rodney found on a newsstand a copy of *Variety,* the national organ of those who sell entertainment. He and his little
niece had no end of fun trying to decipher the strange language which these people contrived for communicating their
special ideas. Pictures were "pix" in the headlines of *Variety,*
because space was precious. When you read the statement,
"Hix say Nix on Mix Pix," you were supposed to understand
that people in small towns were no longer interested in movies
about cowboys and outlaws. Elizabeth had to get busy
learning this new lingo because they were hoping to find news
in this paper about their two little friends and it would be a
terrible thing if they should read it and not understand it!

They reached Chicago that evening. In their hotel rooms
they had another conference with Smith and Guggins. They
heard the ideas those worthies had thought out and told them
their own. They agreed that a showman who had just committed the crime of gnome-gnaping would be expecting detectives after him and would be very careful whom he dealt
with just then. So crude approaches would be worse than
useless. It was agreed that the Chicago office of the detective
agency should send out a woman operative to try to make
the acquaintance of some stenographer in the Quaxton office.
It was agreed that Smith should get acquainted with various
show people and learn all he could about the Quaxton business and its employees. Guggins would set out to learn all

about county fairs and other places which might be interested in exhibiting dwarfs.

Rodney and Elizabeth again registered "incog." It was no longer a joke so they had reasonable-sounding names and were supposed to be from New York. Rodney took it for granted that the gnome-gnapers had been watching them in the Missouri town, so they kept out of sight and spent their time collecting facts about show business from magazines and newspapers and by using the telephone. In the evening Smith came in with a fairly full report about the Quaxton enterprises, including the fact that the showman had a troupe of freaks, with such things as a fat lady and a bearded one, a couple of dwarfs and a five-legged calf, which he exhibited as a side show at various places where big crowds were expected. "I'll be surprised if your Bobo and Glogo don't show up some day with that troupe," said the operative.

The woman detective followed Quaxton's secretary to the place where she ate lunch, and struck up an acquaintance with her. Since the secretary didn't know that her boss had committed a crime, she had no reason to be suspicious. The woman detective posed as a buyer for an out-of-town store. She made a date with the secretary and took her to a show and incidentally heard chitchat about show business. The detective said that she had a friend who was in that business and in course of time introduced her friend, Mr. Smith, to Quaxton's secretary.

So little by little the detectives wormed their way into the affairs of the man. They learned that Mr. Quaxton had a new "attraction," which he was keeping a secret even from his secretary. And before long they learned that his attraction was being taken care of by Charlie Willowby, Quaxton's helper, on a little place which he had in the country. In the meantime Guggins also heard about this attraction, and tried to rent it, to be shown at a country fair in Kentucky.

Smith pretended that he had been to school with Willowby, as a boy. "Old Charlie," he called him and offered to drive the secretary to see him on Sunday afternoon.

They drove to the farm and learned that Charlie had been there, but had left the previous day for parts unknown. Smith was disappointed and the secretary said she would be able to find out in a day or two where he had gone. There was bound to come a telegram or a phone call or a letter.

Rodney and Elizabeth, getting these reports every day, thought that the detective business was worth what it cost. But a couple of days later they discovered that it wasn't worth so much as a morning newspaper. Reading the paper over his coffee and toast, Rodney gave a sudden exclamation: "Here's Bobo!"

Elizabeth caught her breath, and held it while Rodney read a brief item from Johnstown, Pennsylvania, to the effect that at a fair which had opened the previous day there was on exhibition a dwarf who claimed to be the smallest human being ever known. He was exactly fourteen and one-quarter inches high, and yet was a perfectly formed boy and chatted intelligently with anyone. He was the adopted son of a well-known dwarf, Flossie French, who had kept his existence a secret because she did not want him to make public appearances until she considered him old enough. The crowds which swarmed to see him the first day had very nearly swamped the concession that was showing him.

"Oh, do you really think that's Bobo?" cried Elizabeth.

"Could it be anybody else?"

"But where's Glogo?"

"I suppose they thought it was safer to begin with one at a time. You see, they've given him a mother—I suppose to make him a child—maybe they hope to keep legal control of him."

"Oh, Rodney—they can't do that, surely!"

"I don't know what they can do. They must have some idea because they can't expect to keep us from finding him sooner or later."

Rodney phoned the two detectives and told them what he had read. They were to come to Johnstown with him. He might need witnesses or a bodyguard—who could say? The two men, of course, wanted to see the dwarfs, about whom they had heard so much. Rodney told them they would have their thousand dollars apiece, even though he had been the one to read the newspaper first. That cheered them up not a little.

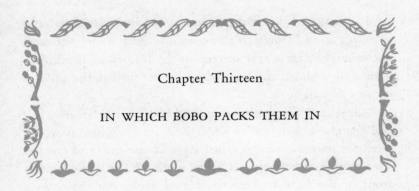

Chapter Thirteen

IN WHICH BOBO PACKS THEM IN

The two cars set out, and two days later were at a crowded city in the mountains of Pennsylvania, built along a narrow valley where two rivers come together, and where the hills are filled with coal mines and blackened with the smoke of steel mills. The fair was held in a meadow quite a distance from the city.

Once there, it was easy enough to find Bobo. It cost fifty cents each for tickets to the grounds, and ten cents more to see "the smallest living human being in the history of mankind." It was a street given up to sideshows, known as the Midway. It had a big tent with signs painted all over it, showing the smallest living human being, in comparison with Tom Thumb and others of the small ones. There was a wide entrance, with several ticket takers, and several other openings for exits.

You had to wait some time to get in, for there was a line all the way down the Midway. They were "packing them in," as the troupers phrase it. The "spielers" were shouting, "Don't be discouraged, ladies and gentlemen, the line moves fast and it moves often. Don't go away until you have seen the most marvelous spectacle ever offered in the history of mankind." Men walked down the line selling tickets so that the throngs could move right in.

Rodney and Elizabeth, with their bodyguard, fell into line and bought tickets and waited their turn. When they entered the tent they saw a raised stage at one end, and on that a large table covered with a velvet cloth. There was a rope in front of the stage to keep the crowd back. No chairs were provided; the people just stood and waited.

Suddenly the curtains at the back of the stage were parted, and a man in gold and scarlet livery came out, bearing a little tray. On that tray stood the smallest of living human beings. There was a murmur of amazement, almost unbelief, from the crowd—handclapping and cries of applause and delight, as the tiny little man stepped from the tray onto the table, and came forward bowing and smiling.

It was Bobo, all right—Bobo dressed in his little brown jacket and short trousers, seeming quite content and at ease, a perfect little "trouper." "Ladies and gentlemen," he said, in his tiny piping voice—the crowd could not have heard him, but a microphone and sound-amplifier had been provided and the sound filled the tent with generous volume.

"Ladies and gentlemen, it makes me very happy to be here and see so many kind and friendly faces. You are surprised, of course, to see such a very small person as I am. But I assure you that I am just like any big person. I am able to think and feel like you. Of course, it is a little hard to be so tiny. I have never been able to go out on the street like other chil-

dren, but here I am, happy to talk to you and tell you about my life."

And so on. Bobo didn't really tell very much, but he bowed, made gestures, laughed and sang a few words. There was enough of everything to let the crowd see that he was real and that he knew what he was doing and saying. When he finished, there was great applause and the flunkey, who had been standing behind the table, extended the little tray. Bobo stepped onto it and was borne back behind the curtains. Then the "spielers" started in, "This way to the exits, ladies and gentlemen. Please move quickly, because there are others waiting to get in to see this marvelous spectacle. Don't fail to tell your friends to come and see the smallest of living human beings."

Rodney and Elizabeth and their bodyguard went out with the rest and sought a quiet corner of the fairgrounds to talk things over.

"It looks as if Bobo has not been frightened, but persuaded," said Rodney. "He seems to be enjoying it and it may be what he wants to do."

"Oh, surely he won't want to stay away from us!" cried Elizabeth.

"We haven't much to offer him, except to take him back to the redwood forest and I've felt for some time that he doesn't want that. We couldn't take him and Glogo home with us—we should be mobbed by reporters and by crowds, as you have seen. We have to be prepared to have Bobo choose a life for himself."

They agreed upon a course of action. They would buy tickets and see the show a second time, as many people were doing. They would get up in front and when the speech was nearly over, Elizabeth would duck under the rope and run up to Bobo and greet him. "They won't be apt to interfere with a child," said Rodney, "and we three can be ready if they do."

"What do you want me to say to him, Rodney?"

"Just talk to him. Say whatever comes to you. Ask him how he is and if he wants any help from us. Tell him that if anybody has mistreated him to say so and we will stand by him and keep him safe. If he's been frightened, make him understand that he doesn't have to be."

What a role to be assigned to a little girl who had been brought up in the most particular society, and taught never under any circumstances to make herself conspicuous! What would poor Mama have said if she could have been there? Or if she read about it in tomorrow's newspapers? But somehow Elizabeth forgot about Mama and was thinking only about Bobo. Mama wasn't in any trouble just then but Bobo might be.

She stood at one side, close to the rope, but hiding behind big Mr. Guggins, so that Bobo would not see her too soon. At the proper moment, just as her little friend was finishing, she slipped under the rope, and climbed upon the platform, crying, "Bobo!" He stopped and gave a cry of delight: "Elizabeth!" She caught him into her arms. What a time they had hugging each other!

It made a grand addition to the "act"! The crowd couldn't be sure whether it was real or just a part of the show. The flunkey in gold and scarlet uniform stood, completely bewildered. Presently two other men came running out from behind the scenes. At the same time Rodney and the two operatives slipped under the ropes and approached the stage, watching attentively. But nobody seemed to know quite what to do about it. Elizabeth went on hugging Bobo and Bobo went on hugging Elizabeth, the two of them pouring out their happiness.

"Oh, Bobo! We've been so frightened about you!"

"I was frightened too. But very soon I saw it was all right. The men didn't mean any harm."

"They haven't mistreated you, then?"

"No, no! They're showmen. They just want to make money."

"And you—you're happy then?"

"I was waiting to hear from you. Did you get the letter?"

"What letter?"

"We wrote to Rodney at his home in Seattle. I didn't know where else to write! I supposed you'd go back there."

"No, we were trying to find you. Oh, Bobo, we've missed you so!"

"Well, it's all right now. Here we are. Where's Rodney?"

"Here he is," said Elizabeth. There was nothing for Rodney but to climb up onto the stage. Bobo commanded it. You could see right away what had happened—Bobo had found out his power. Bobo was the world's greatest theatrical attraction and Bobo had to be kept in good humor, otherwise there would be no more shows this afternoon, thank you.

Men are different from girls. They don't grab each other in their arms and hug and kiss each other, but they have ways of showing their gladness all the same. Rodney shook hands with Bobo and patted him on the back—with one finger—and said, "Hello, old trouper! How's things?" And Bobo answered, proudly: "Well, you can see for yourself! The gate is about a thousand dollars a day and we're splitting fifty-fifty."

"You don't mean it!" said the lumber scion, awe-stricken.

"You bet I do mean it!" said Bobo. "They tried to beat me down but I had it out with them. I get my share, or I lie down in my basket like Glogo."

"Where is Glogo?"

"He's over at a hotel. You know how it is with him—he doesn't like show business. I'm so glad you came, Rodney, and you, Elizabeth, because you are the only ones who can help him. He's not at all well and yesterday he had a fainting spell."

"Oh, dear!" said Elizabeth. "Poor old Glogo!"

"We've done everything we can for him," said the grandson, "but it's no use—he just says he has lived too long."

At this moment one of the showmen ventured to intervene. "We can't get the tent empty," said he. Bobo, practical and efficient, replied, "Quite right. Let's go back behind the curtains. I want my friends with me."

Elizabeth carried him behind the scenes. There was a small rear tent, with several canvas chairs, and for Bobo a table which took the place of his room, having a doll's chair upon it and a basket with a pillow in it. Everything had been fixed nice and comfortable and the smallest of living human beings invited his friends to make themselves at home. Mr. Smith and Mr. Guggins were introduced and on the other side, Mr. Charles Willowby—

"Oh, dear old Charlie!" exclaimed Rodney. "Did you know that Mr. Smith went to school with you?"

"No?" said Charlie and gazed at the "operative." "I'm sorry, I don't seem to remember you. Where was it?"

"Mr. Smith is a friend of Quaxton's secretary," persisted Rodney, full of mischief.

"Oh, indeed."

"We went out to your farm to call on you last Sunday but you had just left."

"I'm sorry," said Charlie. You could see he was beginning to get rattled.

"And Mr. Guggins here," continued Rodney, "is arranging a contract with Mr. Quaxton for an appearance of Bobo at a county fair in Kentucky."

"Well, well!" said Mr. Willowby. "How interesting."

"You see we've been moving right along with you, Charlie."

"So it seems," said the showman, now badly rattled.

An attendant came at this moment to report that it was time for the act. The flunkey presented the tray for Bobo to stand on, but Rodney intervened. "Wouldn't you like to have Elizabeth carry you on, Bobo?"

"Oh, lovely!" said Bobo. "Would you?"

"I'd love to," said Elizabeth. So the smallest of living human beings was presented to the crowd by a little girl, and right behind the curtain stood three able-bodied men to make sure that no one made any move to carry off that precious mite of life.

When that "turn" was over and while Bobo was chatting happily with Elizabeth, Rodney drew "good old Charlie" aside and had a plain talk with him. To make things easier, he said at the outset that all they were concerned about was Bobo's welfare, and if this show business was what Bobo wanted, it was all right with Rodney and they would let bygones be bygones. That cheered Mr. Willowby greatly. He didn't know the legal penalties for gnome-gnaping, but he feared they might be heavy.

He hastened to make clear that they were doing everything in their power to keep Bobo happy and satisfied. If Mr. Sinsabow and his niece would help them they would be grateful. They needn't have the least idea that anyone was being cruel to the little people or keeping them frightened, because, said good old Charlie, "You soon learn you can't get anywhere that way in show business. Whether it's men or animals or what, they don't work good unless they're happy."

"I want to know that Bobo is protected in all his rights," said Rodney. Again Charlie hastened to reassure him.

"There don't anybody need to bother about that little businessman, Mr. Sinsabow. I don't know where he found out about it all, but he sure laid down the terms. He had the boss fairly tearin' his hair before the deal was made. 'No cash, no show,' said he, 'and if you don't play square with me, I'll just tell the first audience and they'll call in the police.' So what could we do with him?"

"Well, well!" said Rodney. "I'm glad he's so competent. Where is the contract?"

"He wouldn't sign anything. He just said he'd work from day to day as long as he got his share of the cash. How the heck did he find out about show business?"

"Well, he's been asking me questions about everything on earth," said Rodney, "but I must say I didn't realize what use he meant to make of it."

"Well, believe me, he knew," replied Charlie; "and he sure did make use of it. He's goin' to be his own boss and have plenty of money and everything he wants in this world."

Bobo came behind the scenes again and apologized for not having more time to talk to his friends. "The show must go on," said he. He asked them if they would go and see his grandfather and try to cheer him up. "We stop for an hour at six o'clock," he said, "and then we can have a real chat."

Rodney hinted that some effort might be made to carry Bobo away, but Bobo laughed at that. Quaxton and Willowby were making too much money out of him. They would stay right here and try to get him to sign a long-term contract. But Bobo had been waiting for Rodney to come, so as to advise him. "I've got to learn to read better," said he, "and I've got to learn to handle my money. There are all sorts of things I want to ask you about. You know how it is, Rodney. People will always want to see me and it's only common sense to make them pay for it and have attendants to take care of me. I've got to live in the world now. I'm no longer a wild thing in the forest and you can bet I'll never be it again. No more hiding in tree stumps for this little gnome!"

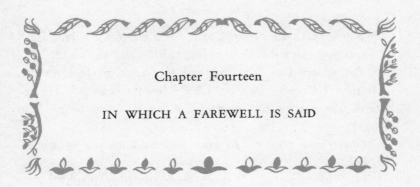

Chapter Fourteen

IN WHICH A FAREWELL IS SAID

Rodney and Elizabeth went to the hotel, where Glogo was being cared for by Willowby's sister. There wasn't much to be done, for the thousand-year-old one just lay in his basket, while Miss Willowby read movie magazines. Poor old Glogo—the neurasthenia had won completely and he just shut his eyes and let it do anything it pleased with him.

He started when Elizabeth spoke his name and opened his eyes and tried to sit up. Yes, he was very happy to see them. He had been sure they would come, but feared they would be too late. Then he had to lie back again for he was feeling very feeble.

"Glogo," said Elizabeth, scolding him, "I don't believe you are getting proper nourishment."

"I haven't much appetite," said the old gnome.

"But you shall be made to eat, Glogo."

"Why should I? What is there for me to do?"

"We're going to find some more gnomes," ventured Rodney.

Glogo smiled feebly. "It's kind and good of you both, but

you know there is no chance of it. The gnomes are done for."

"But you can't just lie here like this!" cried the child.

"You've tried to fool me, and I've tried to fool myself. But now I have to face it. I have lived too long." He repeated the words, his voice dying away, "Too long! Too long!"

"Don't you want us to take you back to the redwoods, Glogo?"

"No," he answered. "I don't want anything at all."

There was a long silence. Then Elizabeth, determined to make conversation, said, "We've been to see Bobo."

"Bobo has found what he likes," said his grandfather in a whisper.

"It really was about the only thing he could do, Glogo." This from Rodney.

"I know. I'm not blaming him. I don't like it, but I'm not going to be here to know about it."

The neurasthenia had won. Glogo closed his eyes again and everything was still.

They tried to think of something cheerful to say but it was difficult. At last they heard a feeble whisper from the basket. "You have both been good to me and I thank you for it—with all my heart I thank you. But now you cannot do any more. I am too tired to talk. Say good-by to me."

It was a command and they had to obey. The tears ran down Elizabeth's cheeks—for she felt sure those were the last sounds she would ever hear from the old gnome. "Good-by, Glogo," she murmured, and touched the withered and weak old hand, already turning cold.

"Good-by, Elizabeth. Good-by, Rodney," said the faint

voice. They tiptoed out of the room, and went back to the world of men who had not yet lived too long—or at any rate did not know that it was so.

From six o'clock to seven the side show closed, for Bobo wasn't going to work himself to death at his first engagement, he said. He had ordered supper brought in for himself and his friends and his orders were obeyed, for Bobo was a rich gnome and spoke with that authority which he had learned from the lumber scion. Rodney was at once amused and amazed to see how much the little fellow had managed to pick up.

The performance started again. Rodney and Elizabeth sat

in the back tent for a while and chatted amiably with good old Charlie. They had come to a tacit understanding to treat the late gnome-gnaping as having been a mistake. Charlie hinted a desire to know where and how Rodney and his niece had met Bobo and Glogo but Rodney said it was for Bobo to tell what he pleased about himself.

In the midst of this chat came a message from Miss Willowby telling them that old Glogo had faded quietly away in his basket. Rodney and Elizabeth had been prepared for this —the thousand-year-old one had practically told them to let him die in peace. Now Elizabeth sat with tears in her eyes, while her uncle and the showman discussed the practical aspects of the funeral of a gnome. They agreed that they would not tell Bobo until ten o'clock, when the show closed. Mr. Willowby suggested the idea of a state funeral, which would bring two or three hundred thousand people to the fairgrounds. Rodney, however, put his foot down, saying that he would have nothing to do with exploiting the corpse of poor old Glogo, who had despised show business and all the affairs of moneymakers.

Good old Charlie finally agreed that that was the right way to look at it. They would bury Glogo without any fuss. He wondered if they had to have a burial permit. Rodney ventured the opinion that gnomes are not recognized by law and the most sensible thing to do would be to take him in the basket which had been his bed and bury him under some great tree, which he had loved. At ten o'clock, when they told the news to Bobo, he agreed with that. Rodney and Elizabeth had been his grandfather's real friends, he said, and they knew what he would have wished.

So that midnight the basket was carried out from the hotel and a funeral procession of three cars drove out into the country. Rodney was driving one, Guggins a second and Charlie a third. They stopped when they came to a lovely place in the mountains. A moon shone dimly through the trees and it was still and solemn and full of the forest odors that Glogo loved. One of the show people had brought a shovel and they found an ancient elm tree and dug a deep hole. They set the basket down in it and stood with bared heads.

None of them knew what kind of funeral service was proper for gnomes and Bobo couldn't help them. So Rodney just made a little speech, saying that their old friend had been a creature of the forest and had wanted to go back to the forest and now the forest would take him to its bosom. Before they quite realized it, Rodney was saying some verses.

> Build his bones into a tree,
> And his blood the sap shall be;
> And his tiny hands shall turn
> Into waving fronds of fern;
> All the forest things that run
> With an old gnome shall be one;
> Every bird shall be his heart,
> And the flowers shall have part
> In his wisdom, and the bees
> Bear his love upon the breeze,
> And the longing of his soul
> Make the fallen forest whole.

So the funeral was over. Charlie told Rodney what a nice poem that was and Elizabeth agreed—she always did, about her uncle's poems. The men put the shovel back into the car and were ready to start. But suddenly Elizabeth gave a cry: "Where's Bobo?"

Bobo was gone! They turned on the lights of the car. Elizabeth got their flashlight and ran here and there in the woods, flashing it and calling aloud. But no Bobo!

She was beginning to get into a panic when suddenly from a little clump of bushes she heard the familiar voice, whispering: "Hush, Elizabeth!"

She stooped down and whispered, "What is it, Bobo?"

"Walk straight away from the others—out into the woods. I must speak to you."

She did as he said. Presently, out of sight of the men, the little one joined her and said, "There are gnomes in this place."

"Oh, Bobo! You don't mean it!"

"I smell them. Everywhere—a whole troop of them!"

"Oh, where are they?" Elizabeth was "excited to death"— it happens to girls frequently and doesn't seem to hurt them.

"They won't come out while you big people are here."

"What do you want us to do?"

"I must have time to look for them. I want you all to go away and leave me here."

"At night, Bobo?"

"Night is the time of gnomes. Will you come back to this place in the morning—early?"

"Of course, Bobo, if that is what you want."

"Tell the others I want to spend the night with the spirit of Glogo. You can tell Rodney about the gnomes when you get him alone, but the others must not have any idea of it. They would come out here and try to capture the gnomes for a show."

"That's right, they would!" exclaimed Elizabeth. How smart Bobo was and how quickly he had learned about men!

"Don't let the men come here with you in the morning,"

he added. "Just you and Rodney. If others come, I won't reveal myself."

"All right," she said. "Do take care of yourself. I hope they are good gnomes."

"I don't believe there are any bad ones," said Bobo. "It is only men who are bad."

Elizabeth went back to where the others were searching and called them together, and said, "I have just talked with Bobo. He is hiding and wants to spend the night here with the spirit of Glogo."

Charlie was dumbfounded. "Is this a trick?" he cried.

"I don't know," said Elizabeth. "I only know what Bobo told me to tell you. He made me promise to come back early in the morning and said that nobody is to come but me and Rodney and that if anybody else comes he will not reveal himself."

So there was a fine mess for good old Charlie! He was furious, but what could he do about it? Rodney said to him, "I assure you, Mr. Willowby, this is all news to me. It is some whim of Bobo's. You know how he is—he must have his own way."

"But we've got a show there, Mr. Sinsabow, and people will be storming the gates."

"Well, if he should be missing for a bit, it really wouldn't do any harm. You could say it was gnome-gnapers—and think what a tremendous sensation it would make! You know—such things have happened."

That was a mean shot and good old Charlie did not fail to get it. "What are you going to do about this?" he demanded.

"Once more I assure you, I don't know a thing about

Bobo's intentions and I don't believe my niece does. Do you, Elizabeth?"

"Not a thing," said Elizabeth earnestly. "Bobo just whispered to me that we must all go away and Rodney and I were to come back early in the morning and nobody else with us— if anyone else came, he would not reveal himself."

"So that's that," said Rodney. "Bobo is going to do whatever he wants and we are surely going to back him up in it."

"And where does that leave me, Mr. Sinsabow?"

"I think it leaves you to wait until tomorrow. You certainly haven't the least chance of finding Bobo in a forest— because he and his people have been hiding themselves for thousands of years, perhaps millions. He will do what he decides."

There wasn't much more to be said—just the same thing, several times over, until Charlie was satisfied that it wasn't doing him any good. He and his men got into their car and waited until Smith and Guggins got into theirs and Rodney and Elizabeth into theirs. Each group was suspicious of the others, each wanting to be sure the other did not stay and find Bobo and carry him off!

As soon as Elizabeth could talk to her uncle without the others hearing, she told him the thrilling news that Bobo was on the trail of gnomes. Then Rodney understood what it was all about. Of course, he was delighted, for that was the real purpose of their trip. He said it was a fortunate thing they had kept the two detectives with them; there might be need of their services in the morning. "We're not going to have any more gnome-gnapers!" he declared.

181

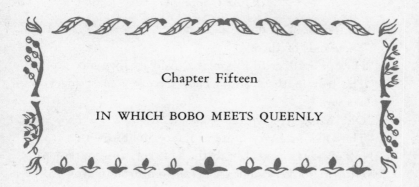

Chapter Fifteen

IN WHICH BOBO MEETS QUEENLY

Elizabeth was so excited she could hardly get to sleep that night. When the hotel clerk rang the telephone bell at five o'clock in the morning, up she bounced, and if it hadn't been for the solemn promises she had made to Mama, she wouldn't have stopped to clean her teeth. They didn't stop for breakfast, but hurried down into the lobby, where the faithful Smith and Guggins were on hand. The two cars proceeded out of Johnstown, Pennsylvania, long before the sun got over the mountains; indeed, before the valleys were entirely light.

They came to Glogo's grave and there Rodney set the two men to watch the highway, with instructions that if Willowby or any of his men came in sight, Rodney was to be called. Then he and Elizabeth went into the woods, as nearly as they could to the place where Bobo had spoken with Elizabeth. There they called him and before long heard his answer. They found him, hidden in a clump of the beautiful wild laurel which is so plentiful in these forest-clad mountains.

"I have met some gnomes!"—such were the little fellow's first words.

"Oh, Bobo! You don't mean it!"

"Thousands of them!"

"How grand!" cried Elizabeth. "And are they nice people?"

"The best in the world. They have the most marvelous civilization."

"Oh! They are civilized gnomes?"

"They live in a city quite as fine as Johnstown."

Now Rodney and Elizabeth had got an impression of Johnstown as a very smoky city, uncomfortably crowded between the hills, but they didn't want to hurt Bobo's feelings.

"How perfectly thrilling, Bobo!" cried the girl. "Did you see their city?"

"They took me all over it."

"And may we see it, Bobo?"

"I'm sorry about that, Elizabeth, but you see these gnomes have never let big people meet them—that has been their law ever so long. I fear I can never persuade them to trust big people with their secrets. In fact, they didn't want me to come away again for fear I might betray them."

"Oh, Bobo, how terrible! I'd have died if you hadn't come back!"

"Well, I finally persuaded Mr. Morgo—he's the great capitalist who owns their steel plant."

"Good gracious!" exclaimed Rodney. "Do they have steel?"

"They live in these mountains which are full of both iron ore and coal," said Bobo, "so why shouldn't they make steel?"

"It's quite an operation," replied the other. "I'm deeply interested to learn about it."

"Sit down and I'll tell you," said Bobo.

The forest was damp this early in the morning, but the

thoughtful Rodney had brought the rug, also Bobo's basket with the thermos bottle. They spread the rug and sat down. Bobo said he would sit in the mountain laurel, on the chance that dear old Charlie or somebody else might intrude upon their talk.

Their little friend unfolded to them the amazing story of his night's adventures. Following his sense of smell, he had found the cleft in the rocks through which the gnomes come forth, and making his way in, had come to a series of caves which contained the city of Gnomestown, with its coal mines and steel plant and factories. Of course, there had been great excitement on his arrival. The chief of police had been summoned and had escorted him before the mayor, who in turn had notified Mr. Morgo, the banker and capitalist of the gnomes. Bobo had spent most of the night interviewing these gentlemen and another one with a long white beard who looked amazingly like old Glogo, and turned out to be the bishop of the Gnomic church, diocese of Pennsylvania.

"Were they polite to you?" asked Elizabeth anxiously.

"Oh, indeed!" replied Bobo. "You see they were excited to meet a California gnome."

"Oh, then they know about California?" inquired Rodney.

"Who doesn't know about California? It seems that their ancestors came out of the redwood forests, millions of years ago. They have written records of it and pictures of the giant redwoods."

"How interesting, Bobo!" cried Elizabeth. "And how terrible that we can never see all that!"

"I don't think you would enjoy it so much, Elizabeth. You see, the caves are very low in places—they are all right for gnomes, but you would ruin your clothes and you might even get stuck in some place and they would have to dig you out. And then, too, it's rather depressing at the moment—you see, they are in the midst of a spell of hard times, and there are many unemployed and much suffering!"

"Oh! Then they have the business cycle in Gnomestown also!" exclaimed Rodney. "How very surprising!"

"I assure you they are up-to-date in every way," said Bobo gravely. "In fact, they have many inventions about which man is only beginning to learn. They don't have to come out into the forest to gather fern seeds any more. They make what they call synthetic foods—do you know that word?"

"Oh, yes," said Rodney. "Our scientists know of such matters."

"Well, they make their foods out of coal tar, and really, they are delicious. They are a most healthful race of gnomes."

"Except those who are sick, I suppose?" inquired Rodney.

"Oh, naturally," replied Bobo. "But they don't count those."

There was a pause. Then Elizabeth wanted to know, did they have lady gnomes? Bobo answered, "Of course," and that was the most wonderful thing of all for him.

"You see, Elizabeth, I had never known any other gnome but Glogo. My mother died when I was a baby and the others disappeared one by one before I was old enough to pay attention. When Glogo and you and Rodney talked about lady gnomes, it didn't really mean much to me. But now—oh, it was the most amazing experience!"

"You have met one, then?"

"I have met the loveliest creature—she is really very much like you, Elizabeth—only about seventy years old and has fair golden hair and lovely kind blue eyes and she wears a dress of bright blue synthetic material which they make out of coal tar, like the foods."

"Who is she, Bobo?"

"She is only daughter to Mr. Morgo and lives in a lovely palace and drives around in the dearest little sports car you ever did see."

"And was she nice to you?"

"Well, you see, Elizabeth, it's not good taste for me to mention it, perhaps—"

"Oh, don't mind!" insisted Rodney. "We're old friends and we must know about your welfare."

"Well, you see, it's this way—coming from California and having seen the whole United States pretty nearly and been in a circus and in the newspapers and all that—it made me something of a hero to them, as you might say, a romantic figure. So I think I can say that Queenly Morgo—"

"Is that her name, Bobo?"

"Don't you think it's a nice name for the daughter of a captain of industry and finance? Well, anyhow, what happened was that he begged me to come back and marry his daughter."

"Oh, how sudden!" ·

"That is what I said. But you see, they were terrified that I might betray them and the big people might capture them all and put them in circuses. On the other hand, they were afraid not to let me go, for fear that you might make a search for me. So when they decided to trust me, Mr. Morgo took me aside and said that he would make me his son, and teach me the steel business and I would fall heir to his estates, and perhaps I could help him to solve the problem of—what is it you call it, Rodney?"

"The business cycle."

"And did you accept his offer?"—this from Elizabeth.

"Surely. What else could I do?"

"Of course, Bobo—it's exactly what we have all been looking for. Only, naturally, we thought you would find forest gnomes and live an outdoor life."

"I know. But times change and we have to adjust ourselves."

"I think you have made a very wise decision, Bobo," said Rodney. "And I hope that you and Queenly live to be happy ever after."

"And won't we ever be able to see her, Bobo?" asked the girl.

"It'll be a little hard to arrange," said the other gravely. "You see, these are people of importance and, just as on earth, they have to watch out for gnome-gnapers. But when they have got to know me better, they may be willing to trust my judgment of my friends."

"How shall we ever meet?" asked Rodney.

"I've been thinking about it. If you would be willing to travel to Johnstown, say, one year from this date—"

"Oh, surely, Bobo!"—this from both Rodney and Elizabeth.

"Well, then suppose we say that you meet me at Glogo's grave, exactly one year from the hour when we buried him. I will be there and perhaps I can persuade my wife and her father to come with me."

"All right," said Rodney. "It's a bargain." Then, after a pause, he said: "I suppose you wish to hurry back to your bride."

"Thank you," said Bobo. "That is very considerate of you. The truth is, they are fearfully anxious lest I change my mind and not keep my promise."

"Good-by, old friend," said Rodney, and held out one finger for Bobo to shake.

These two masterful men did not show their emotions. But Elizabeth began to weep—however, she hastened to explain that part of it was because she was so happy for Bobo.

She had to bend down, and the little gnome came running out from the laurel clump and gave her a hug—of course, he couldn't hug the whole of her neck, but he did the best he could and kissed her on the forehead and shook several of her fingers—a grand time they had, bidding good-by there on the mountainside above the Conemaugh River. The last thing they saw as they went was a tiny silk handkerchief waving out of the clump of bright pink laurel.

Rodney had to drive back to town and pay off Smith and Guggins and thank them for their help. Then he had to break to good old Charlie the heartrending news that the smallest of living human beings would not be available for exhibition any more. They didn't tell him what Bobo was doing. They just said that he had decided not to return to the circus. Of course, Willowby thought that Rodney and Elizabeth had stolen his treasure away, but there was nothing he could do about it and very little that he could even threaten.

Rodney telephoned Mama that they were on their way home and they set out, taking the northern route because it would be cooler. It took them through the State of Minnesota again. Every time Elizabeth saw cows on Bobo's side of the car, it made her lonesome. They had Bobo's basket in the back and all his things in it. She meant to keep them always, for a souvenir of the journey of the gnomobile—which, of course, was no more a gnomobile, but just a common car again. It was that way with everything—the glamour had gone out of the mountains and lakes and forests, filling stations and picnics and hitchhikers and all the happenings of the highway—now that there were no little creatures in the back seat running from side to side and asking questions.

It was the same way in their home state, Washington—a country with plenty of rain, and in the great Cascade range no end of forests. The highway passed a point of land, high up, commanding a sweep of mountains, chain beyond chain, with trees so thick they looked like the fine pile of velvet. They got out to admire this sight and Elizabeth exclaimed, "Oh, Rodney, how Glogo would have loved this!" Then she added solemnly, "When I grow up, I'm going to help to save the forests and have them all full of lovely little gnomes again!"